# PRAISE FOR
## *The Sunday Tertulia*

"Heartfelt, intelligent . . . imagine Amy Tan's *The Joy Luck Club* crossed with Laura Esquivel's *Like Water for Chocolate*. . . . Carlson's love and appreciation for Latin cadences comes through on every page."

—*Los Angeles Times*

"A winner . . . imaginatively written."  —*USA Today*

"Charming. . . . *The Sunday Tertulia* is entertainment, a lovely froth of anecdote, advice, and philosophy."

—*Chicago Tribune*

"A charming, wise, and inspirational first novel . . . earthy, yet spiritual."  —*Publishers Weekly*

"Carlson's first novel is a delightful story about female friendships and the trials that life brings to us. . . . [It] captures those special feelings that stem from being with and trusting close friends."  —*Booklist*

# The Sunday Tertulia

# The Sunday Tertulia

### Lori Marie Carlson

Perennial

*An Imprint of* HarperCollins*Publishers*

A hardcover edition of this book was published in 2000 by HarperCollins Publishers.

First Perennial edition published 2001.

*Designed by Sherri L. Hoffman*

Library of Congress Cataloging-in-Publication Data is available.

ISBN 0-06-095367-5 (pbk.)

01 02 03 04 05 ❖/RRD 10 9 8 7 6 5 4 3 2 1

*For my mother, Marie Elaine Carlson, and my friend,*
*Beatriz López-Pritchard*

*Who said that a room*
*of one's own was enough?*
*Why not enchanted gardens,*
*palaces of memory,*
*houses of language?*
    —MARJORIE AGOSÍN,
        *Lluvia en el desierto*
        (*Rain in the Desert*)

# Acknowledgments

$\mathcal{T}$he inspiration for my novel has been the *tertulia*, which is a cultural tradition among Spaniards, Latin Americans and Latinos, and, also, my beautiful Latin American/Latina friends. My portraits of Pedro de Valdivia and Inés de Suarez are shaded by fantasy, but the story takes its cue from the very finely researched history, *Pedro de Valdivia: Conquistador de Chile* by Ida (Stevenson) Weldon Vernon. I am indebted to Ms. Weldon Vernon for all details relating to the particulars of Pedro de Valdivia's and Inés de Suarez's meeting and voyage to Chile from Peru, as well as their establishment of Santiago. The poem, "Vanilla," on pages 46–49 is from the collection *Generous Journeys* by Marjorie Agosín and her permission to use it in my work is deeply

*Acknowledgments*

appreciated. The Nahuatl poem excerpt, which I have translated from the Spanish on page 194, is from *Historia de la literatura hispanoamericana, Vol. I,* by José Miguel Oviedo. All Cervantes citations are from the Tobias Smollett translation of *Don Quixote de la Mancha.* Many thanks to the Bobst Library of New York University and the New York Horticultural Society Library. My profound gratitude to my husband and to my family; they have been there from the beginning with love and encouragement. I also thank two former professors, Olga Impey and José Miguel Oviedo, for their enthusiastic support of my writing when I was in graduate school. Harriet Wasserman added magic to my adventure. And Lyda Aponte de Zacklin and Carol Hoffeld were the first readers. The intelligent guidance of my agent, Jennifer Lyons, kept me moving along. And, then, Joëlle Delbourgo graciously opened the door. My editor, Julia Serebrinsky, took me many steps further, allowing for better perspective. My work has been influenced by them all.

*Preface*

$\mathscr{E}$very month or so on Sunday afternoon, Isabela, whom I often think of as my adopted aunt, has a festive *tertulia* lunch in her airy Arts and Crafts apartment on Manhattan's Upper West Side. A *tertulia,* by nature, involves a lot of thinking out loud about everything. Our lunch is basic fare: a hearty *arroz con pollo* or some other Caribbean chicken and rice dish, accompanied by red beans, yucca in garlic oil, lemony avocado salad, and dessert. Although the food is good, the company is better.

There is Aroma, a world traveler who happens to be an excellent gynecologist and Mexican down to her purple-polished toenails. And the brainy Sonia, an Argentine by birth, who never fails to entertain us with her encyclopedic knowledge of literature and history, whether or not we want to hear it. "*Chicas, chicas,*" she might say, "did you know that ancient Romans used to hang white roses from the ceilings in their homes? Blos-

3

somy white blooms only, which meant that any conversation in the room was strictly confidential, or 'sub rosa.' Maybe we should do that, too."

Another beloved member of the group is Luna, a Peruvian chef, and what a chef she is. Her meat turnovers are remarkably succulent because she always adds a jigger of *pisco* liquor to the filling. Pearl, who is a Bolivian American and a painter, flies to New York every chance she gets to be with us. And Winifred, an elegant landscape architect from Chile, manages to attend, oh, probably once a year. Whether with regulars or occasional visitors, the conversation circles around the same beguiling topic: the wonderful, confounding, and difficult aspects of life. *Nuestra vida.* Steering our conversation through laughter and tears, a few angry outbursts followed by a heaping spoon of dark chocolate cake drenched in caramel or, if we are very lucky, sweet-corn ice cream, is our hostess, Isabela, forever calm and gracious, quiet and dignified, insistent in her counsel. And admired by us all.

I happen to be the only gringa among us, and the youngest. This may be a fluke, but I like to think of it as destiny. When I came to Manhattan just after college, I brought one suitcase packed with summer clothes and grandiose notions about my future. Some said I was a perfect Alice in Wonderland, a flaxen-haired, wide-eyed dreamer, always soaking up possibilities from literary tomes.

My family say they never saw me without a book when I was growing up. As a teenager, when given the choice of going out with friends on Friday nights or staying home to read, I'd almost always choose the latter. Back then, the nineteenth-century British writers were my favorites. I adored Thomas Hardy. Absorbed in tales of moors and mysterious castles by the sea, I would look up every once in a while through the large window in the living room to the woods beyond our house. Always looking beyond. Wondering what kind of life I might have if I left my sheltered town of Prendergast, New York.

And this is how I came upon the notion of a future in New York City. At first it was just a hint. A feather of a dream tickling my imagination. The possibility of speeding toward something powerful. I sought adventure, exploration. New York beckoned with its endless avenues, chance encounters, and whirlwind of people and ideas.

I didn't know a soul when I arrived that summer after college graduation. Cautiously, I made my way along the flower-laden sidewalks on the Upper East Side, strolling through the Guggenheim Museum or the Met or a bookstore on Fifth Avenue on my solitary weekends. I didn't have a job, or any promising connections. And I was living in someone else's apartment. My summer sublet was a small blue studio in a brownstone that had once been Alma Mahler's. A neighbor told me so one day as she was walking by. I thought it was a happy omen, suggesting that my life could be extraordinary, carved out of vision and desire. Then there was another auspicious coincidence: Gloria Steinem lived in the adjacent brownstone.

When I told my mother that the editor of *Ms.* lived next door to me, she was thrilled. She viewed Gloria Steinem as a modern-day heroine and I suspect something of an urban fairy godmother. One weekend, when I was home for a visit, she nervously admitted that she had written to her about helping me find an apartment of my own. Before I could let Mother finish her story, I cried, "How could you?" "But you know what?" she answered with a tender smile. "She wrote me back, Claire." And then she waved a white envelope before me. Inside was a handwritten letter in which Ms. Steinem offered assistance, if I cared to stop by her office.

I tried to explain to Mother that she shouldn't worry so. She stared at me incredulously. I rattled on and on about my hunches and daydreams. I was convinced that I should be exactly where I was, regardless of how very unsettling my beginnings in Manhattan might appear, and I was determined to make Mother understand.

In moments like those, it helped to remember that my best friend in college, Lucy, a warm and spirited Mexican, respected my faith in the magnetic force of destiny. She used to have similar feelings about being able to intuit one's direction in life. She once told me that the human body does not end at its extremities; it ends with agitated energy, a few inches from the corporeal frame. Fields of light. That's what we are, she would say with deep conviction. Moving globes finding paths through time and space.

Just after I returned to New York, following that brief stay home, my sixth sense directed me in a way that would change my life. One very warm afternoon, I felt the urge to go to the Brooklyn Botanic Garden to see the extraordinary roses I had heard so much about. In my loneliness, those first days in June, I often went to public places on the weekends just to have some company. But that day I felt a particular pull, an unusually strong desire to heed my inner voice.

I remember my encounter with Isabela in that garden of wide lawns and shady paths as though it happened yesterday. Soothing color splashed around me. Banks of tangerine, red, fancy yellows. Pink. With pen in hand, I was writing down short entries in my journal about them all, magnificent old-fashioned roses, the kind of roses that are found in European country gardens: the Damask, Gallica, Centifolia, and Moss.

Isabela and three of her best friends, although I didn't know it at the time, happened to walk by the bench where I was sitting. A sudden breeze lifted a sheet of paper from my lap and Isabela rushed to catch it. "What are you writing, dear?" she asked me, curious yet proper, her smile outlined like a prim teacup.

I had detected a slight accent, and before I knew it we were making small talk. Just hearing the Spanish musicality of Isabela's English and watching her move with an Old World elegance made me think of some of my favorite Latin American college professors, aristocratic in their bearing and maternal in their concern for their students. The others offered courteous introductions, too, all the while nodding their hat-covered heads in complicity and showing off the most exquisite hand-painted fans.

When I remarked that I spoke Spanish, eyebrows shimmied all around. Were they surprised because I didn't look Spanish or Mexican or Chilean? Or that I spoke their language with authority? Probably a little of both. Mind you, Isabela, a Cuban-born Puerto Rican, doesn't look Latina either, what with her light blue eyes and wavy red hair.

I've always thought stereotypes about what *looks* Latin or American or European are wildly inaccurate. This goes for temperaments, too. When I studied Romance languages in college, most of my classmates were much like me, distinctly North American but possessed by more Latin fire than Yankee coolness. We couldn't wait to connect with others just like us, wherever they happened to be in the world.

Before I knew it, Isabela, her pals, and I were heading toward a coffee shop. At last, that fortuitous summer afternoon, I had found my first real friend in the city.

Quite soon, I became part of Isabela's coterie. A group, interestingly enough, that reflected the diversity of Latin culture: Caribbean, Southern Cone, Andean, and Mexican. A Pan-American group.

A retired pharmacist, Isabela, I soon discovered, was known in professional and social circles as "a mover and a shaker." She knew people in every corner of the city and seemed to have made friends with everyone for whom she ever filled a prescription. But her real circle of trusted confidantes was surprisingly small, and she guarded her privacy with care.

At first, she would invite me to her apartment for tea and cake, sometimes a glass of Santa Catalina wine. Then, toward the end of summer, she asked me to her Sunday lunch *tertulia,* the inner sanctum of her social life.

The women, all of whom I'd first met in the rose garden, just delighted in the fact that I knew so much about their world. And when I told them I had attended *tertulias* in one form or another since my high school days, they seemed even more impressed. It was the beginning of a beautiful, almost religious breakthrough for me—maybe for them, too—that we could have such camaraderie even though we did not share the same cultural heritage. Much more important, we simply got along. We were women,

10

first and foremost, with the same fears, problems, and challenges.

Without my asking, Isabela helped me find a job and a permanent place to live. I recall mentioning that my sublet was up at the end of the summer just once to her. The next thing I knew I was moving into a surprisingly affordable one-bedroom with parquet floors and fleur de lis molding around the ceilings—owned by yet another friend of hers and rented to me as a favor. Weeks of countless interviews with headhunters had come to nothing, and then she called a friend of a friend and suddenly, I was working as a paralegal in an international law firm in midtown. I had finally found a place from which to launch my aspirations.

Although my salary is still at the low end of adequate and I'm not crazy about my womanizing boss, my office on the thirty-seventh floor has a view. A magnificent view of the Empire State Building, the Hudson River, and no one believes this—a terrace. A place to hide early in the morning, before anyone arrives at the office, so I can plant a bed of dahlias in the summer and a few small evergreens in the fall, to remind me of home. A place where I can go, with my coffee cup in hand, and actually imagine for a minute—between a thousand business calls and lawyers yelling for a fax, "Claire, *pronto, s'il vous plaît, bitte, bitte*"—that my dreams of greater accomplishment will come true.

It has been several years now since I've struggled in New York City, and instead of getting easier, it seems that my life has become more complicated. "Just don't you worry; everything will turn out fine," says Isabela, as the room around me seems to swim in tears, my own. Sometimes I am worried about a member of my family or upset about some guy I've dated, and usually I can't scrape together the money for my rent. Almost always I'm just too overworked and can't think straight. But the blessing in my New York life, a very rare gift, is the *tertulia.*

When I'm at Isabela's house I find real comfort. In the form of words of wisdom— knowledge gleaned from years of living and making mistakes and learning the ins and outs of interacting with one another, sometimes hurting, sometimes helping, she tells me in her unmistakable, pocked voice. I listen while I watch her drink a cup of very sweet—four teaspoons full of sugar—*café con leche* and I lean back in the rocking chair, listening and thinking.

Soon enough whatever bothered me when I entered her apartment is forgotten.

That is why we all come to her sun-drenched, book-filled home. It is a place of genuine humor, serenity, and affection.

Gradually, I have come to rely on the opinions of the women at Isabela's *tertulia,* all of whom have benefited from a rich and open approach to life—like the forget-me-not sky of summer afternoons. I think of them as fragrant bouquets of joy and *alegría.* Truly generous. My friends and advisers. Strong women whose histories are lively and whose counsel is intelligent.

I don't always agree with their opinions. Sometimes I may not like the tone of their voice or "where they're coming from," but, over the years, I've learned that I'd better listen carefully, because a whole lot of living has become the music of their spirit. And the rhythm is good, as powerful as *cante jondo.* As Isabela so often says to me and everyone she meets, *"En el camino andamos, y en él nos encontramos."* (As we journey along, we discover who we are.)

# 1

On an Autumn
Afternoon

After five years of living in Manhattan I realize there is nothing more beautiful than an afternoon in mid-September, when the sky is the color of lavender and the light behind the clouds is opalescent, heavenly. Everything in the city comes back to life in autumn, and that includes the *tertulias* in Isabela's apartment. This is the first one of the season, and after so much traveling in August, we are anxious to catch up. I'm the only one who didn't go away; as usual, I didn't have sufficient funds. So, whether I intended to or not, I explored my city and learned a little more about it. For instance, where to go to escape the suffocating pollution that drapes every corner (the Boat Basin off Riverside Drive at 79th Street), how to sleep in a room whose windows are painted shut, without air conditioning (with ice-soaked towels covering legs and stomach and a fan), what to eat on next to nothing (iceberg lettuce chopped finely with a carrot, cucumber, and a slice of turkey), and even where to go to meet nice men (definitely the eleven o'clock service at almost any church; my preference is Riverside).

Our Sunday afternoon ritual of catching up invigorates the pace of our month. We gossip, recount favorite stories, and I get an earful of advice. There is a lot of teasing. The conversation seems to fall out faster than a clip of castanets. We jump from topic to topic so freely that at times I can't tell who is saying what or why. We're just so happy to be back. Meanwhile, Isabela conducts the flow of our voices with the artistry of Zubin Mehta, using her solid hands to bring one of our voices higher or lower, depending on which is more in tune with her way of thinking. She definitely has a few ideas about my most pressing concern of the moment: I just can't seem to get ahead in my career. No matter how hard I work, or how much effort I put into all the aspects of my job, nothing changes the fact that

I'm still a paralegal making very little money. I keep asking myself how this can be. Wasn't I the girl about whom everyone would say, "Claire, you'll be a star someday"? In college all my diligent work led to success. Excellent grades and praise from professors. I was good with people, a manager and leader. Involved with student government, I had a flair for bringing disparate groups together on campus, fraternity brutes and overachieving scholar types, students whose worldly airs rubbed Middle American innocents the wrong way, the joiners of every club and committee and the loners who studied on Saturday nights in the library basement. And I believed, that's the thing, I really believed that I would be recognized outside of college in the very same way. I thought that being a woman in our enlightened society would be no different, in terms of achieving success, than being a man.

So how can I explain why my boss said recently, "I can't give you a raise on your good looks, Claire," when I asked him for a modest increase in my low salary? I had just been given someone else's job—coordinating assignments in the translations department of the law firm—in addition to my own. The guy who had this responsibility before me was being paid twice as much as I am now, and I have two jobs to do. Never in my wildest dreams did I imagine that my gift for languages and ability to speak Spanish, German, and French would get me into trouble in such a tony law firm.

On my way to Isabela's, I am still furious thinking about that sexist comment. It seems to me that when a woman is young, people tell her that she lacks stature, that she's too inexperienced to be taken seriously. As she grows older, they say she shouldn't complain too much about work ("Be nice!") because there is so much competition from younger women bubbling over with energy. My heart aches at the thought. Isabela and her friends, of course, always have a way of setting me straight, telling me to buck up or eat right or concentrate on the positive. Isabela, especially, seems to thrive on offering her opinions.

*Isabela* ⟶ Claire, my dear, if you want to get ahead you have to fight; otherwise you'd be sitting in a chair doing

20

the same thing all your life. Yes, yes, you know that. But by fighting I don't mean being aggressive in your conversation or your actions. You can fight by using your charms. A smile here, a smile there. Being a good listener, asking questions. Knowing how to dance can't hurt, either. I think a woman needs a little *angel* and a little *duende* to get by in this world. You need to be sweet and you need to be hot as a jalapeño. *Así, lo es.* Nobody, for example, can charm people like my cousin Celinda and at the same time get exactly what she wants. And she is so smart! When she left Cuba, she couldn't take anything with her, just the clothes on her back. But Celinda had an extremely good idea. She gathered together all her Colombian emeralds and her sisters' diamond jewelry and had the jeweler in her town take the stones from their settings. But how to smuggle out this wealth without arousing the suspicion of the authorities? She had to find a receptacle of sorts that no one would dream of looking into or coming near. Do you know what she did with all those stones? She put them in her baby's dirty diapers! When they were at the airport and the officers were checking everyone, not one of them would come near her baby, Alejandrito, that day. In fact, those big strong men were pinching their oh-so-sensitive noses. Celi and her sister really had to stifle their giggles as they boarded the plane to go to my Tío Práxedes' house in San Juan. But more important, Celi—through her intelligence—had outfoxed those bullies and she was able to rent a nice apartment right away with the money she got for all her jewels.

*Luna* ⟶ Obviously, Celi is a clever woman. But if you ask for my advice it's prayer, constant prayer, that makes a life extraordinary. Recognize the power of God to help you, Claire. *Ay, sí.* I say this prayer each day: "*Señor, Señor,* all-powerful Father, generous Father in heaven, please help me in everything I do. That's all *and* enough. I think of all gifts the good Lord gave women, nothing, absolutely nothing, can take the place of *esperanza.* Hope. *¿Sabes?* When I was a young woman, Claire's age, there were so many times when I wanted to give up certain dreams because my chances looked bad. Worse than discouraging. And if it weren't for the values my family had taught me when I was young, I would have forfeited a college education and career. Values like perseverance, patience. I didn't have money to do what I wanted but I did have hope I would somehow earn it. I was eighteen when my papa died. I knew that I'd have to find work in order to earn the money I needed for school.

22

And so I got two jobs to pay my way, one in a fruit and nut shop on 67th Street and the other in a French bakery. It was tough—I was exhausted and discouraged because I had no one to help me. Most days I didn't feel like getting out of bed. *Ay, sí.* How could I study when I had just worked six hours straight? But I did it, and now I have a future. It's important to keep sight of your goals, no matter what they are. But without the ability to imagine goodness and light ahead of you, nothing comes to fruition. *Esperanza, esperanza, hermanas.* And the saints in heaven at your side.

As I listen to Luna mention saints, my mind begins to wander. I wasn't raised a Catholic and, truthfully, all that talk about little painted statues enveloped in a gilded light seems odd to me. And there are way too many of them. How can she, or anyone else for that matter, keep them straight? Ita, Darsius, Scholastica, Polycarp for the months of January and February. Braulio, Cuthbert, and Patrick in March. In April, Fulbert, Alferius, Hunna. And on and on. Granted, they have intriguing names and often unbearably harsh life stories, but I can't see how invoking their pres-

23

ence during life's daily trials could really help me. And yet when Luna, who is so persuasively faithful, talks about the otherworldly power of saints in our lives, I want to believe that they could actually come to my rescue. I need all the help I can get.

*Aroma* ⁓ As all of you know only too well, anything I've ever gotten in my life through hard work began with a lot of faith in myself. My prescription, ladies: Dream every morning and every night. Twice a day. I had never thought seriously about the energy behind our thoughts, the power of desire, until I was sixteen or so. I remember I was sitting in the airport, waiting to take a plane home to Mexico from Los Angeles. I was reading a magazine when a professorial-looking man came over and sat down beside me. He introduced himself and asked me what I was reading. He must have seen that I was crying. I told him it was an article about achieving personal goals. I guess I was battling a case of the blues because everything seemed to be going wrong. It looked like my parents would be separating. I had few friends in the private school I was attending. I didn't care for my teachers. And because I felt so little support around me, I had started feeling really hopeless. I was losing my confidence. Nothing felt certain to me, and I was scared. "It's not enough to have dreams in your heart. You have to put your heart in your dreams," he said, and patted my back. "It's that simple." And you know, he was right. From that day on, I realized that if I wanted to be a physician, I'd have to believe that I was already a doctor—that I was born to be a doctor. No one or nothing would stop me. I willed myself to hope.

*Isabela* — But, *mira,* getting ahead in life can't compare to contentment. Happiness comes from within, not from having, but from being. It depends mostly on being able to recognize the positive around you, Claire; that is what counts in this life. Don't forget. I'll tell you a story. There was a woman once, someone I knew socially, not so well but well enough, who had a terrible case of arthritis. It had penetrated her hips, her feet, and her hands. Her fingers were swollen and gnarled like, well, how would I describe them . . . like tough grapevines, I'd say, and many times she cried in pain. She told me something. *Escucha bien, eh.* She said, You know, Isabela, I thought I'd live my life in constant agony, but one day I decided to try to overcome this and I began to do volunteer work. My priest suggested it. So I went to the local hospital and they gave me jobs like reading to elderly patients, visiting sick children, taking flowers to the cancer ward. Well, the result was amazing. I stopped thinking about my arthritis and my pain. I started feeling peaceful just bringing a little joy to people. A child smiling at me when I rubbed her back and sang a song. Reading aloud a letter from someone's son who lived thousands of miles away. Small acts such as these that I was asked to do as a volunteer. And do you know, the pain really disappeared.

*Aroma* ⁓ Ladies, think of your health. Now, good health is happiness. Of course a little hanky-panky with a handsome man can't hurt. No, a lot of hanky-panky.

**Aroma does not mince words. It's always sex, rice, and beans. She even gives advice to her patients about the art of seduction. What to wear in the evenings, what perfume to use, how to coo in bed. She seems to get as much pleasure from talking about the act of making love as doing it. Maybe it's her profession. Doctors are different. So matter of fact in their descriptions about the body and its functions.**

*Luna* — I find happiness when I'm in church. Peace surrounds me there, the organ, *las oraciones, el cura,* the warmth of stained-glass windows, candles beneath St. Jude's statue. Comforting reminders of the divine. Ay, Claire, let me tell you, there was a time when I was very unhappy. I was running around. Going to clubs. I was always anxious—worried whether a guy was going to ask me out, wondering if I'd ever marry. I saw my friends, one by one, getting engaged. I spent more time trying to be a matchmaker for everyone else; that's why I married late. My friends would call me up to say, "Luna, can I spend the night at your place, José and I have had a fight." In time I realized I was pretty lucky. I have tranquillity and I learned to depend on myself. And all my friends, I think, see it, too—because they keep asking to come to my apartment. *"Ay, Luna, me siento bien aquí,"* they say. *"De veras, me siento bien."* Look, every day give thanks for what you have. Simply count your blessings from above and one by one you'll see just how rich you are. Compassionate friends in whom you can confide and from whom you receive encouragement. An open heart. Every day, gratitude. Then joy seems to slip into your life. And this joy can lift the spirits of those around you. *Ay.* Perhaps only as the years go by can we really understand the true meaning of happiness.

When I was a child I'd love to visit my grandparents on their farm. It was in northern California. I can still remember sitting on a swing, gulping lemonade that my *abuela* made from fresh-picked lemons, honey, crushed ice, and mint. Swinging back and forth. Swinging. Slowly sipping that sweet and sour drink and listening to Grandpa tell his stories. That was happiness unlike any I have known since then. It is really pleasurable to recall those days and imagine myself in the back yard of that old white house. I can just about capture the moment, if I try really hard to remember the details—how cold and slippery the frosted glass felt in my sweaty palm, the scent from Grandma's sweetpeas, her habit of coughing twice after telling a joke. Focusing on those two special human beings can make a bad day so much better for me.

I agree that happiness is anywhere you find it. Running in the park, seeing friends, going to a party. Luna, I think, has got to be the most religious woman I have ever met. Almost everything she does has a mystical dimension. How is it possible to nurture spirituality in a city so driven by the material? Even the others in our *tertulia* say she isn't practical enough. Isabela often laments, "That Luna, she's flying in another orbit somewhere. Where did she come from, anyway?"

Sometimes I worry about her, too. She just doesn't seem to realize that her attitude is out of sync. On second thought, I take that back. I remember once she told me about an incident involving a woman who hired her for a party. A smug psychotherapist. As soon as Luna walked into her kitchen she met with a barrage of insults. Apparently this shrink thought she was pretty hot stuff. She told Luna she didn't have self-esteem, that she ought to live her life more aggressively. She hadn't even met Luna before. Luna told me the word *ugly* came to mind as soon as that lady opened her mouth. So odious, so arrogant. Yes, that was it. Luna said, "Claire, that woman was harsh and, so angry inside. I don't think she had a clue about the power of the human spirit. She certainly didn't understand me. I felt like running away from her as fast as I could." Then Luna said something to me I will never forget: "Claire, those are the kind of people I pity. They simply can't see. They impose their own poor vision on the world around them with such certainty, it's frightening."

Luna often talks about God as her source of deep, quiet strength. She may appear to be fragile, but it's really her way of being strong. Because she understands humility. She would never think to boast about herself. Luna may be the strongest woman I know. Because she doesn't care how others view her. She knows who she is. "And that is enough, Claire," she tells me. *"El Señor* knows who I am."

*Isabela* — My friends, *"Camarón que se duerme, se lo lleva la corriente."* (The shrimp that sleeps is carried away in the current.) When all is said and done, the most important element of success is the hard fight that takes you one step further. I think the way you go from being a young girl with a heart full of hope to the woman you want to be, when you might have people telling you that you're not good enough, or that you're aiming too high, or you don't have what it takes to make your dreams a reality, is simply by having unshakable faith in yourself. Once you realize that mean criticism has to do with the way others feel about themselves, it's easier to shrug your shoulders, brace yourself against hostility, and go full speed ahead. Never, ever listen to someone who tells you that you are not worthy of your ambitions. Tell them to leave you alone. Because no one, *repito,* no one in this world needs discouragement.

Now, Claire, here is a story especially for you. A long time ago, I knew a beautiful girl, a girl who had so much ahead of her. In fact, she was so smart and decisive she could have achieved much in the way of power; she could have become the president of a bank, or the mayor of her town. She married a young man with whom she had fallen in love, and thinking that he wanted her to develop her talents, she started little by little to put her trust in his ideas and judgments. Unfortunately, he was more concerned with controlling her than he was in making her feel happy. And, my goodness, that poor girl, within a very short time had no faith in her abilities. Instead of saying, *I can,* she started pleading, *Can I?* And this girl's husband always said the same darn thing: No. Well, the situation became so awful that this young lady, who was once confident and charming, started to stutter terribly. To this very day, I remember her saucerlike eyes—alert and open—fading to gray as she tried to communicate her feelings or ideas in uncertain, halting words. It was terrible. Yes, that stutter was a heartfelt cry. She was so roped off from anything nourishing inside her that she couldn't speak. I will never forget her look of loss. I will never forget how she let herself become a puppet because she didn't keep her own sure faith. No, *señor,* I cannot forget her.

Certainly, it's nice if a woman finds a partner and marries. No one really wants to live alone. And yet I don't think marriage is wonderful, at all, if a woman has to give up her career or her very unique dreams for a man. That's plain *estupidez.* Any woman who thinks that she can sit back and watch her life as though it were a parade while her husband pursues his goals is just plain foolish. Besides, with divorce being so prevalent, a woman never knows when she'll need to really dig in.

Permit me another story. I had another dear friend, Mia, who married a man she didn't love. Her parents wanted her to marry a doctor, at any cost. *Dios mío,* that man put her through hell. Pure misery. He didn't want to work, he didn't work, and when he did, it was frightening. I was always afraid something or other would go wrong, because, you see, he drank. There was Mia with nothing to do but worry sick that there would be disaster for one of his patients. But she never said a thing. Night after night, day after day, Mia sat in her big house … just frozen. How could she have gotten into such a mess, I kept wondering. Of course, in those days, women like myself didn't challenge our parents too much. And when her papa decided she should marry this good-for-nothing, she did. "But, *papi*," Mia kept saying, "this man is a drunk! "No, no, *mi hija,* he's a good man," he replied enthusiastically. "He comes from a fine family. A doctor. He will make you happy." On the surface, at social gatherings, of course he was a gentleman, a sophisticate of sorts. But remember that old saying, *"Candil de la calle, oscuridad de la casa?"* (The life of the party, the downer at home.) He fooled just about everybody. There was nothing she could do, and so they married. *Bueno,* all that is behind her now. What saved Mia's life was her father's farm. Because, you see, she did divorce that piece of *mieeeeeeércoles. Pues, ¡claro!* Mia left him one rainy night and kept walking, walking, walking till she opened the front door of her father's house. "I'm home and I'm not going back," she announced. And that was the end of that. They got a divorce. Two years later, her papa died. And she was left with a dairy farm she didn't know a thing about. But Mia was determined to run that creamery. And so every morning, she got up at three o'clock, way before the roosters, and I swear, she learned by dint of desperation. Oh, I think she must have cried every morning as she lugged all the pails and buckets from the back porch of the house to the barns. She hardly had time to eat—maybe a little bread or banana or a piece of cheese—while she was hauling or shouting orders to the workers. But the old foreman, René—a man in his eighties—took care of her. Taught Mia everything she had to know. He was so patient. A miracle, a real saint of a man. And now the dairy farm is so successful she can travel anytime she wants, go anyplace she wishes. And better yet, she isn't passing the time with a man who soured every waking moment of her existence.

**Sometimes I feel as though I'm hearing much, much more than I bargained for at our *tertulia*. The way Isabela tells it, life is fraught with danger at every turn. And the only way a woman has**

34

to get through her earthly days is by having the strength of an Amazon. I just want to be treated fairly for what I do. Is that too much to ask, I mean, is everything a struggle? Isabela would probably answer yes. But with one of her proverbs. *"El hombre propone y Dios dispone."* (Man proposes, God disposes.)

# 2

*On Sonia's Birthday*

$\mathcal{O}$f all the birthday gifts I have ever received, my favorite is the complete works of William Shakespeare. A present on my thirteenth birthday, from my parents. When I was young I liked the love sonnets most. I remember one especially, Sonnet 54, which alluded to the concept of internal beauty. Shakespeare made an appeal to my tender teenage heart. He challenged the notion that physical perfection is a woman's most important asset in life when he claimed:

> *O how much more doth beauty beauteous seem*
> *By that sweet ornament which truth doth give!*
> *The rose looks fair, but fairer we it deem*
> *For that sweet odour which doth in it live.*

Now, Sonia, whose birthday we are celebrating with Moët & Chandon and carrot cake smothered in cream cheese frosting, baked lovingly by Luna, is a woman who never let her beauty dictate anything. She's not the type to go to salons or get her hair done. In fact, she told me once she has never had a facial or a manicure. And yet she is startlingly lovely. I think we admire her not only because she is so intelligent, but because she lives her life ambiguously, on her own terms, not deferring to the limitations of a world in which men still try to define femininity for us.

One thing about Isabela's friends is that they are strong, emotionally and physically. When any of us has a birthday, the talk inevitably turns to food, secret ingredients, exceptional cookbooks, like Nitza Villapol's *Comida criolla,* and the value of good nutrition. And how many times can Isabela say she likes beans—I can't even begin to count, but here she goes again.

*Isabela* ⟶ *Compañeras,* although I do like chicken and it's simple to prepare for lazy cooks like me, I guess I forget

**40**

how many really tasty dishes I can make with beans. For example, chorizos with garbanzos. I found this recipe in a little booklet once, and, well, I think the dish is perfect for a birthday lunch, especially in autumn. And since I know our Sonia likes spicy food, I've doctored it up with chili pepper. I buy my chorizo at the Colorado Market, you understand; they have the best meat in the neighborhood. The butcher is Argentine. He always saves the best cuts of meat for me. Of course you have to play a little Gloria Estefan when you cook, or maybe some ballads by Plácido Domingo. The music helps the cooking along. No doubt about that.

**None of us would deny that the Colorado Market has the best meat in the neighborhood, but personally I think Isabela has a crush on Mr. Argentina. It's more than a hankering for his steaks and chicken. Which reminds me. I wonder if she has ever been invited to a *parrillada,* a real get-down-to-earth Argentine barbecue. I have to admit that I love the juicy, salted steaks from the pampas, but I could do without those crispy, crackling mallow delicacies, like cow testicles.**

*Aroma* ⁓ *Bueno, bueno*, beans are more than opening a can and emptying them into a pot, along with everything else. *Dios mío.* You have to be adventurous and delicate with beans, I tell you, Isabela. I love you, I respect you, but enough is enough. After all these years I should think you'd learn to make them in an elegant, more imaginative way, a way them lets them show off a bit. Let them be the star at the table, instead of third cousin. Beans aside, I always say if you are going to make chicken—and what's better than a Sunday chicken—prepare it without the skin. Remember your health. Healthy food for a healthy heart. Why, I would never eat a chicken with its skin. No, no. And you have to add *cosas buenas*, like parsley, onion, a lot of garlic, carrots and potatoes, mushrooms, sometimes peas. You have to add a whole garden to a chicken to make it taste really, really good. In my home, we didn't eat so many beans. And to tell you the truth, I've never been a bean eater. And whenever I cook a Sunday chicken, I try to dance a little in the kitchen. I put on the radio, listen to some *salsa* or some *soca* and start moving to the music, hiking my hips and dropping my shoulders—*oooomp, oooomp, así*—in between watching my chicken turn a honey color. It's fun and *muy, muy buen ejercicio.* Excellent exercise.

*Luna* ⟶ Now that we're sharing recipes, I'll give you one that my great-great-grandmother Filomena María Ruíz wrote down for all of us in my family. It's the easiest and the most delicious appetizer you can imagine. *Ay.* Spanish, from Barcelona. All you need is a good loaf of bread, white bread and pretty light in weight, like a baguette. A bottle of your favorite olive oil and two or three juicy red tomatoes, cut in half. Slice the baguette into one-inch-thick rounds, put a teaspoon or two of olive oil on each, and rub the cut tomato on top, so the pulpy liquid soaks through. Sprinkle with a little crushed garlic. Add a shake of salt. It is so good I can feel the insides of my mouth squeeze tight just thinking about the flavor. But I particularly believe in the magic and garnish of herbs. For me, the best is basil. I put it in my homemade chicken soup. My secret ingredient. I also make a sauce, a kind of *ajilimójili,* from cilantro, tomato, onion, and sweet red chilis. All you do is chop the ingredients into slivers, throw in a little salt, add cold-pressed olive oil and a squirt of lime juice, and mix together. It's perfect for meat, chicken, or fish. Sometimes I put it on baked potatoes or rice instead of butter.

*Aroma* ⟶ Herbs, certainly, enhance beauty. Young women, like Claire, rarely think of all the benefits of these slight greens. I grow all kinds in terra cotta pots on my kitchen windowsill. Now, Claire, that is something you can do, too. Even in that pillbox of a kitchen you have. Herbs and herbal teas are very good for the body. Not only basil, but what about mint, oregano, camomile, lemon verbena, and lemon balm, garlic, lots of garlic, sorrel, dill and chervil, bay, parsley, rosemary—for love and good luck, don't forget—thyme, tarragon, and sage. Essential! Herbs keep my thighs trim—and danceable, *te digo la verdad.* True, true.

*Luna* ⟶ There is another herb, which few people know about. *Stevia.* Indigenous to Paraguay. And it is so sweet it's even better than honey. They say it's three hundred times sweeter than sugar, if you can imagine. *Ay, sí.* This is what you do. Take some *stevia* leaves and some rose petals or violets—make sure that none of the flowers have been treated with chemicals—and put them in ice trays with water to make patterned ice cubes for cool summer drinks, like mint julep. I also fill a compote with as many herbs as are in season, winter or summer, and keep them on the kitchen table. Instead of a vase of flowers. They can be every bit as beautiful and fragrant. When I'm cooking, all I have to do is pull a few leaves, snip a bud, and—*iqué maravilla!*

*Pearl* Well, I've always said you've got to use your imagination when you cook. For any chef, the counter and the table are like a painter's canvas. Think: color, scent, and texture. Smell, taste, and touch. That's right. Cooking is like painting. I do believe that anyone can appreciate the appeal of culinary color. The hues of earth and sun seduce the appetite instantly. That's right. I ask myself, Will this purple squash make a nice accompaniment to the oven-roasted duck I am serving? Would I do better to slice small red and white radishes, *me encantan rábanos*, on top of my green salad rather than put them on my antique Mexican clay plate? What color sauce should I streak across this poached Dover sole? A dollop of whipped cream on my orange mousse? The bravery of Picasso! And the aromas of my kitchen are equally important. When my guests arrive, I want them to be greeted by a breeze of marvelous scents— of pickled cucumber, warm cinnamon, rose, chocolate, and vanilla.

*Lori Marie Carlson*

*Sonia* ⟶ Oh, I love vanilla. Anyone know this poem by Marjorie Agosín?

*Vainilla/Vanilla Bean/Vanilla planifolia/Vanilla*

**I.**

*A soft hand*
*dewy, candid,*
*extracted from the deep skirts*
*of the beloved earth,*
*dangling dice,*
*vanilla seeds,*
*clairvoyant gamblers,*
*to place in*
*the secrecy*
*of my ear*
*on my instep*
*with its several swirling aromas.*

**II.**

*Vanilla*
*protectress of the bonds of love*
*of luminous nights*

*of equal love for streets*
*and slopes*
*vanilla like a friendly knife*
*was the epitome of softness*
*of whatever climbs and becomes noble,*
*when it arrives at the delirium of touch.*

### III.

*Vanilla, cousin of cacao*
*elegant and mysterious lady of sonambulant*
    *regions*
*loyal sorceress of sleepless bodies*
*you grow wild and discreet*
*among bushy deserted slopes of the landscape*
*and from afar*
*in alien distances, bony, empty,*
*your scent hovers in the very roundness of the air.*
*From Oaxaca*
*fruitful province*
*where women*
*carry iguanas on their heads*
*as one bearing love, in clearings*
*you appeared*

*before the incredulous eyes of transient intruders,*
*were an exquisite treasure of*
*noble savages*
*like the Duke of Marlborough*
*who carried you to cloudy foggy England*
*where you accompanied shapeless desserts*
*of respectable ladies,*
*but I remember you*
*wild, barefoot,*
*appearing among brambles*
*to teach me*
*the tricks*
*and deceits of tyrannical bosses*
*desire desired*
*and here comes my mother*
*to smooth my skin with*
*vainillón,*
*the wild vanilla of South America*
*from mysterious Oaxaca*
*vanilla*
*elegant and wild*
*cousin to cacao*
*mortal enemy of bitterness*

*everlasting plant of*
*happiness*
*shaped*
*like a*
*knife,*
*you come,*
*you remain.*

Sonia's face unveils so many attitudes and moods as she recites this lovely verse. Her face is as fluid as the sea. This is not the first time I've heard a poem recited during a meal. At the *tertulia* it happens frequently. And the funny thing is, all of Isabela's friends love poetry. For them, verse seems to emphasize a point better than raising one's voice. The real secret of Sonia's beauty, I think, is a combination of her intelligence and the softness of her speech. When she speaks, especially when it's about fine literature, I fall into a kind of blissful stupor. There is a swooshing to her Argentinian accent that can mesmerize. I call her Sonia *de la Voz*. And then when Aroma picks up where Sonia has left off, it's drums and percussion, deliberate and persistent. More and more prescriptions. *Más y más recetas.*

*Aroma* ——◦ Ladies, ladies, in addition to rapturous vanilla, true beauty can be enhanced at any age by good nutrition and exercise. Now, don't you all agree that Sonia is more beautiful today than when we first met her? I really mean that. Her eyes sparkle—a sign of internal balance. I would say she is in good shape. And Claire, even though you are still young, you can get a jump start. For example, eat lots of fruit—*una necesidad.* A prescription, ladies: Fruit juices in the morning and at night. I make *horchatas*, shakes, with fruits like *papaya, piña, coco, guava,* and *chirimoya.* And here's a blender beauty potion. Take a few peeled cucumbers and slice finely. Put these in the blender, add a little water, and blend on high speed. That's it. You can drink the liquid or eat it as you would a soup—with a twist of lemon, salt, and freshly ground pepper. A cleanser for the blood, and so refreshing! Also good: freshly cut-up, raw tomatoes. Of course, a daily regimen of exercise is essential to oxygenate the system. Healthy cells, remember, my dear friends, thrive on oxygen. I myself dance in my apartment, alone and happy, *completamente* happy, to the sound of Tito Puente or if I'm in the mood for tango, a little Astor Piazzola. Or even some merengue. And I do love Juan Gabriel, *mi compatriota*. But I think my best weapon against aging is the forest in my house! When I first decided to buy house plants, I remember the man who convinced me to buy twice as many trees as I had wanted said this: "You'll sleep much better if you put a few trees in your bedroom." And oh, was he right. Not only have I slept well all these years, thanks to my beautiful Brazilian, Chinese, Costa Rican, and Venezuelan plants, but I think my skin has kept its elasticity. It makes sense if you think about it. All that weekly watering goes right back in the air, which ultimately moisturizes my skin. Make your house green, that's my second prescription for the day.

Between my schedule—a workday that begins at eight and ends at eight—lack of greenery in my apartment, and the pollution in New York, I imagine my skin doesn't look too clear or luminescent. And it seems to me that Aroma, good doctor that she is, looks at my face with undeniable concern. Is she studying my wrinkles?

And so it goes on an afternoon of birthday revelry. Not only did I eat delicious cake, cake so moist and creamy that I asked for seconds and for thirds. Sips of champagne, rich conversation, laughter. After such an awful week, I feel restored. A Sunday as simple and sacred as this permits me to face yet another Monday of legal rigmarole. I've started to believe there's much, much more to life than work. Isabela's attractive friends make that point again and again in their inimitably enchanting way.

# 3

## On Jealousy
## at Christmas

$\mathcal{M}$y favorite time of year is Christmas. In New York, especially. I doubt that there are places in the world where last-minute hassle and celebrations blend more harmoniously. Bold, budlike lights on struggling sidewalk trees. Rows of evergreen lend charming definition to Park Avenue. Trumpets and ballet, operatic choirs. And the parties! All the more reason to feel miserable about an unexpected streak of envy that has come upon me. I can imagine my soulful mother admonishing me, "Claire, at Christmas, especially, such feelings will not do."

I have to admit that just a few days ago, at our annual office party, a certain Jillian, another paralegal, had such a sobering effect on me; I still cannot shake it. She walked into the party showing off a sexy cashmere suit. Probably a Dolce and

Gabbana. I have to admit I am a little jealous. The stirrings of this envy began when she boasted about her salary in the ladies room one morning. "I can't believe I'm paid so much for doing just a little research," she offered in that cloying manner of hers. As it turns out, she makes about three times as much as I do, and her workload is half of mine. It bothers me to think that she can buy Italian couture and eat out anytime she wants, while I must scrounge around at bargain shops. If I weren't working so much harder, I'd understand. But every night she leaves at six and I'm still in the library looking up rulings for my lecherous boss. The truth is ... before I started my job, I naively thought if I gave 100 hundred percent, I would be rewarded. Then I see others putting in half of that, and getting back twice as much. Someone told me Jillian got her job through connections, an influential friend of the family. Deep down I know that I should never covet someone else's fortune. We all have our own paths to follow. And I do keep in mind that jealousy is destructive. But I am having

**a hard time getting rid of the nagging question: "Why her and not me?"**

*Luna* ⟶ Dear Claire, *querida*, I am a great believer in the power of prayer to change the heart, as you know. But sometimes, even I have to confess, prayers, just like a decent seafood *paella*, need a little *aioli*, a jolt, to come to life. Aroma, what would you say to Claire about jealousy?

*Aroma* ⟶ That the affliction of *celos* is a woman's worst enemy. It should be tackled fiercely, like any illness. So, a drastic prescription is in order. *¡Claro!* This is an old, trustworthy instruction, which I found in a Spanish book of medieval medicine in Madrid. Thread a few garlic teeth into a necklace and wear it around your neck when you sleep for at least a week. That should kill it most effectively.

**I love these Old World beliefs, and the poetic flair with which they're passed on generation after generation. The concept of jealousy is a subject of peculiar and extensive discourse in Latin culture. It appears in a whole range of folkloric mention.**

Precautions and potions for its elimination are described in countless books of essays and poetry. Latinas, whether they be housewives or professionals, have clung to the practices of their mothers, grandmothers, and great-grandmothers with enormous enthusiasm, unlike so many of us North Americans who are always coming up with our own trendy remedies based on new and vague studies of our emotions and needs. Anything new promises to be better, and we so seldom question such cutting-edge thinking. I admire the convictions of Isabela's friends and how they passionately express and adhere to their heritage.

*Pearl* — *Bueno, chica*, it's easy to be glib if you have a good income. That's right. What if you really don't have money, I mean the kind of salary that allows for good health and peace of mind? It is so hard. I sympathize with Claire. I do. When I was beginning my life as an artist, I went through some very trying moments. Sometimes I didn't even have money for food, so I guess you could say I fasted before it became fashionable.

But it's interesting to try and beat being penniless. At

night, I would make mental lists of every bill I had to pay, and then I had to think up ways to either pay the bills or stall. I was stalling pretty regularly. Then I realized I could do some concrete things to lessen all the financial pressure I felt. That's right. For instance, when I couldn't afford to pay my rent, I would go in person to see my landlord and just tell him very honestly that I didn't have the money. Could he wait a few more weeks, I'd ask, my hands clenched, until I sold a painting to some wealthy banker my agent assured me was just about to buy my work? I don't know whether it was the look of terror on my face or my honesty, but my landlord never said no. Another tactic that came in handy was asking the bookkeeper of the dress shop where I worked days if she could possibly give me an advance on my salary. It had never occurred to me that this was an option, until one afternoon I simply got so desperate for money—I had overdue bills and creditors were calling me; I couldn't afford to go to the doctor or the dentist—that I was forced to ask her if she knew of any extra work I might be able to do. She asked me what the problem was, and then simply offered me the advance on the spot. Maybe I really had a guardian angel looking over me, I don't know. Because, somehow, I always got by.

One night, I was crying so hard my sight was blurry. I had exactly five dollars to my name. I didn't know where I would get the paints I needed to do some work, when I realized that I had a cabinet full of dime store makeup. I took every tube of old magenta lipstick, smoky eye shadow, pale powder, and blush, added a little oil and some water, and went to town. I did miniatures, a series of fifteen sketches that a dealer saw the following week and bought himself for a few thousand dollars. I felt utterly rich. It's when I had so little money that I had no choice but to produce my very best paintings—the paintings that would eventually make me financially secure.

What I learned in all of those desperate moments was not to let fear paralyze me. I was exhausted, blue, from never, ever having money. Month after month, year after year, it was the same. I'm not going to deny that I seemed to have a low-grade depression during that time. I just got by, no matter what I tried. That's right. But as long as I could keep my cool, I managed to create little plans that bailed me out of my predicament. Being poor forced me to imagine better, and I learned to push as hard as I could until all the negatives in the picture became positives, really and truly push myself to the best of my ability.

*Luna* ⟶ If you think about the way so many people live their lives, rushing and pushing and putting up—always racing against the clock—"time is money" living, you start to wonder why. Does anyone need that much to be content or comfortable? I've always thought the real question is not, *How many thousands of dollars can I make*, but, *How well do I live?* When I was growing up my mother and father kept repeating this: Find something you love to do in life—we don't care whether it's dancing, studying law, or making pastry—and put all of your effort into doing it well. Everything will follow if you do this. Money is a tool, a useful tool, because it allows for certain kinds of mobility. But don't live to make the tool.

**I would have agreed with Luna before I came to New York. But here everything is different. Life in New York City comes down to money. Even basics. Like safety, health, and love. Just yesterday, one of the lawyers in the office, a young French guy with a little too much self-confidence for my taste, said he thought that single women aged much faster in New York than anywhere else in the world. "In Paris," he said, "women are**

more beautiful. They make love more, work less."
An exaggeration, of course. But I think I know
what he means. The pace of work and the pace of
just being in Manhattan can wear women down.
Brutally.

*Sonia* ⟶ Actually, I think the worst jealousy is when
you envy someone's dreams. I mean it. I had a friend who
was jealous of my dreams. Can you imagine? Every time I
began to talk about my future plans, she'd change the subject, act as though she hadn't heard a word. Now what
would you say threatened her? Could it be that she per-
ceived I had the strength to make my dreams come true?
And listen to this. Last Saturday I went to a tea at a colleague's house and I had the most disagreeable encounter
with a woman I had never met before. I'm still reeling
from the experience. We started talking about our work
and I mentioned that I was doing well and had received
my first book contract. She looked me straight in the eye
and replied with all the dryness of chalk, "Well, I have
many friends who have tried to publish and none of them
has been able to. You must be successful because you're
good-looking." I swear. And you won't believe this: She's a

women's studies professor! And as if that weren't enough, she apparently had read an article about Hank's latest house design in *Architectural Digest*. Based on what the writer had to say about my honey, she decided he was the man for her. There I was, minding my own business, when she pounced on me. Just as I had managed to gulp down some tea, somebody mentioned the article as a kind of compliment to our romance. *Bueno.* This vile woman shot up from her seat and professed that, in fact, she was in love with my boyfriend based on what she had read. Not only that, she was going to figure out a way to meet him so she could tell him in person they were meant for one another. I sat in my seat like a sack of rice. Everybody looked as though they just had eaten a few raw sea urchins. Then one courageous soul, I don't remember who, said in a tiny voice, "But don't you know that Sonia is his better half?" And then I heard a sound, a cawlike voice, say, "Youuuuuuu! Youuuuuuuu! are my riiiival!!!!!! Well, don't be happy just yet. I still have a chance. You're still not married, are you?"

*Isabela* — *Ay, bendito.* Don't obsess, Sonia. Now, getting back to the subject at hand, which is money. Women

**63**

don't save enough, it is all too clear. I've seen young girls come to this city, get a job, and spend every single penny on this light pink wool suit, or that silver band, or Italian bags and shoes, so that they can look pretty at work. Years go by and then this *muchacha* is in her forties, with a huge closet of clothes and nothing to count on for a rainy day. My father, a banker and a good one, gave me three capital rules, Claire: Save. Save. Save. According to him, income should be divided into three areas of savings: the bank, stocks and bonds, and real estate. And be mindful of utilities. I think it's best to put your money into telephone companies, electricity. Conservative ventures that you can count on.

*Luna* ⟶ Yet I think all of us would agree that jealousy is a terrible emotion. I can't think of anything more insidious in a woman's life. *Ay, Dios.* And so I recommend that if you feel the weight of jealousy, Claire, get down on your hands and knees and . . . pray that it be lifted from your soul. My own, more fanciful antidote to jealousy at Christmas is to decorate. Preferably a Christmas tree. Douglas firs, I think, are most attractive. Decorate with large glass balls to catch the morning light and the late-afternoon sun. Pink and white and gold. And as you hang one here, another there, ask God for a blessing. A Christmas tree in multicolored lights—the tinier the better—with crystal balls will protect a human being from any nasty spirits. But as added protection, I recommend putting two full glasses of water at your bedside to trap those malevolent creatures. *Ay.* Guardian angels help, too, of course.

*Sonia* ⌁ I think it's rather simple. Just ask yourself if anything positive can come from jealousy. Once you hear the irrefutable answer, *no*, within your heart, turn your face to the winter sun. Get on with it. Or as Cervantes would say, where there is an "abundance of grievances to be redressed, wrongs to be rectified, errors amended, abuses to be reformed, and doubts to be removed," we cannot waste time on lower human emotions.

**Sometimes, all we need to hear is what we know to be true from friends whom we trust to mean well. It wasn't easy for me to admit at the *tertulia* today that I was jealous. But it was an energy I clearly had to shake. Discussing problems at a *tertulia* is different from sitting down with my American friends and having a *tête-à-tête* over**

coffee. What I truly appreciate about Isabela and the rest of the group is the intense activity of thought and the love of words that seem to carry us from one issue to another. When we gather, it's not about one person offering a disinterested warning or a few ready-made suggestions. It's better than that. Our meeting has to do with narration in all its forms.

Isabela's chums love to hear the music of language, the dips and turns of poetry, the art of eloquent debate and good, really good, storytelling. Their distinctly different voices come together in a madrigal, catharsis for us all. Pearl's story about being poor has given me something to really think about. I am, all of a sudden, more confident that in the future my finances will improve. As I get ready to face the icy wind lashing off the Hudson, I really do feel better. I walk a little lighter.

# 4

*On Luna's
Broken Heart*

$\mathcal{I}$was doing a little Christmas window shopping not far from where I work when I saw Luna's husband with another woman in a passionate embrace. Although I met Gabriel only once at Isabela's, I recognized him immediately. He is very striking, with salt-and-pepper hair and chiseled features. I looked away, embarrassed. I felt ashamed to be a witness to this public act before me and about two hundred other people on Fifth Avenue, charged with so much private consequence. The woman with him was nice-looking, medium height, brunette, and seemed very expressive. She was hugging him and laughing as they walked past me. Gabriel blushed scarlet when he saw me scampering in the opposite direction with my head down.

Now what do I do? Do I tell Luna or do I keep quiet, I ask myself over and over again as I walk to Isabela's apartment. I sit down on her well-worn couch and notice that in honor of the holidays, she has displayed her collection of *santos* on a long narrow table. These very old eight-inch saint figurines are fashioned from gold and wood and delicately painted. I stare at the Three Kings and begin to tell her about my day—monkey business at the law firm or who is dating whom. But I do not mention what I know about Gabriel. Instead, I complain endlessly about my boss, who has developed the sickening tic of sliding his hand down my back whenever he walks past me. A habit that—as I've already made clear to him— disgusts me. But he does it anyway.

Surprisingly, the following Sunday when we are having lunch, Luna raises the subject of her marriage.

Initially, I didn't realize that she was talking about herself. She mentioned, first, that one of her acquaintances was getting a divorce. But then I noticed that Isabela reached out to touch Luna in a very knowing way. And Sonia got up and gave her a hug. Aroma handed her a handkerchief. Luna hadn't even eaten a forkful of rice and black beans before she started to recount what she knew about Gabriel. In almost predictable fashion, she mentioned the signs that pointed to something going on behind her back. A Christmas card, more sexual than spiritual, left carelessly on his bureau. A phone number scribbled on the inside of a matchbook cover from a midtown club. A touch of lipstick on one of Gabriel's white dress shirts. Then the nights when he would phone her saying that he was running a little late at the office. All of it going on for well over a year. This was more than I wanted to know, but obviously Luna had told her four best friends about her suspicions long before this lunch.

Now that I am part of this special family of confidantes, I guess I should feel privileged that she has such trust in me, too. She leans forward, resting her chin on her hand. I see dark circles underneath her soft hazel eyes. Her cheeks are hollow near the jaw, and she looks, frankly, awful. Women suffer for their love so. It makes me think that we are born warriors. When Isabela tries to cheer Luna up, she just sits back and shakes her head.

*Luna* ⟶ I have to admit, Isabela, I've had better days. Knowing that my husband is a chickenshit, believe me, isn't easy. I have begun to despise him. I really have. And I am ashamed because I always thought of myself as a forgiving woman. I hate myself for hating. *Ay, sí.* I know some of you think that I should weather the storm, swallow my pride, and see if this affair falls apart. But then what? I will have had to use every illusion I can muster to endure the strain, and where will I go for peace of mind afterwards? How will I be able to go past the hurt, even if he leaves Elizabeth? All I can think of is the unfairness. How could he? How could she? I feel absolutely destroyed. And praying, well, praying . . . I really can't this time.

*Isabela* ⟶ At moments like this my mother, bless her soul, would say: *"Manos frías amor por un día, manos calientes amor para siempre."* (Cold hands, love for a day, warm hands, love to stay.) Luna, just this once you must, I think, try to overlook the indiscretion, as hard as it may seem, and go beyond your pain. You've spent too many years with Gabriel to let this affair destroy what you have together. You know, marriage is never easy for anyone. And I think sometimes it's better, well, if a woman looks the other way, pretends she doesn't know what's going on. Elizabeth isn't any better off than you are—you may just find that you have a more solid relationship than you think. Remember: He could have deceived you, never told you about it, but he did!

*Luna* ⟶ Whatever do you mean, he told me? I caught him red-handed. I found a photo of her in his duffel bag, and confronted him. A photo of her nude, remember. *Ay*, some of what you're saying makes sense. But what you don't realize is that I feel as I though I've been pummeled within. I've had to accept the fact that my husband has been having an affair with the hostess of some cigar club. Besides worrying about my health, I'm sick at heart. My insides have been cut to shreds. I feel piecemeal. Bloody. Really numb. So hurt I can hardly get through the days. You don't spend years with the man you love and take his affair lightly, unless of course you don't really love him. And I have truly loved my husband. What's worse is that I feel so emotionally exhausted that I don't know what is logical anymore. I mean, one day I woke up and looked at the man I adored next to me in bed and kissed his ears and gently touched his head, thinking, *My God, what a marvelous human being,* and the next day I found out he was having sex with a woman I wouldn't have lunch with, and I thought, *My God, what a fool I am, what a wretched, blind woman,* and I didn't know who I disliked more, my husband, his lover, or myself. And now I feel the bile coming up inside me every morning, and I just can't stand it. I burn inside and I want to run so fast and hard that I'll lose myself forever.

*Ay,* maybe the only way to act well in all of this is to be the stoic. But how can I come out of this mess intact? Even if I leave him for good, I don't think I will ever be whole again. It's not as though the two of us sat calmly down and decided "time out." He's been taken from me, just like an amputation. We're joined by so many memories, so many happy moments, and even sadness. But we're joined. And then I often wonder about Elizabeth. She obviously doesn't give a damn about me, my feelings. What does that say about us women? Can we possibly be sisters in a world where we constantly fear our love is fair game for someone who wants a piece of it? The heart of the matter is: If a woman does not have respect for the sanctity of another woman's marriage or relationship, how can we go out in the world and be enthusiastic about each

74

other? I have never wanted to hurt a soul in my entire life. I couldn't think of coming between two people who are attached. And I don't mean to sound self-righteous. I'm just trying to understand how any woman could do this and consider herself a friend to women. Look, attractive men have flirted with me, asked me out—and in moments when I could have used a little happiness, a little badly needed attention—but I said no. We can say no, that is an option. So I must be missing something.

*Aroma* ⟶ Well, as a doctor devoted to taking care of women's private parts, this is how I would explain the situation, Luna. Women who have affairs with married men simply make themselves forget that their lovers have wives. They are so needy. If they could picture the anguish on those wives' faces, maybe they'd think twice about it. In other words, they don't even rationalize. They don't care. They think of their pain, their loneliness, and try to rid themselves of it. And it doesn't matter to them, at least at first, if their lover is attached, as long as their immediate needs are met. I admit, this is pretty bleak. But I imagine they probably don't see their relationship that way. Otherwise they simply wouldn't accept such a mess. And, of course, I'm sure that some women like the challenge; they get satisfaction from the competition of it. An ego-booster.

And I'd be less than honest to tell you that I am guilt-free. I once had a dalliance with a married man. We interned together, and we were both young. I know it sounds bad, and now I know it was stupid, but then, well, I didn't stop to think. He made himself so available, and he was so good-looking that I just couldn't resist. I don't think that it went on for long, maybe six months. What changed everything for me was meeting his wife. It was an accident. A colleague at the hospital had a party one night for all of us interns, our dates, and our spouses. And my friend thought I wouldn't be going. I remember when I walked into the dining room to have a drink, there he was, holding her hand, and oh, I just felt so small. And that was the end. Look, Luna, the truth is this: You cannot control the man you love and you can only determine how you will live, not other women. So, you see, we must be strong, ladies. You must have courage, Luna. And if you can't be brave right now, we will be brave for you.

**Aroma always seems to find just the right words for the occasion. And I can see that Luna feels a**

**little better already. Something about Aroma's outlook is so even-keeled and compassionate. And she is honest.**

*Pearl* —— I don't think any of you know this, but Ricardo and I almost divorced a few years back. What happened between us changed my life forever. And I'm not saying that all couples should handle a crisis similar to ours the same way, but it's how we were able to put our lives back together. What happened was that Ricardo was teaching a course at Firebird and one of his students, a very beautiful young woman—I'd say about twenty years old—started to flirt with him. At least, that's Ricardo's version of the story. But why not? He's a handsome, sophisticated man. Anyway, the two of them began to meet after class and one thing led to another and, before he knew it, he was sleeping with her. In the afternoons. So, you see, I didn't suspect anything for a long, long time. What hurts me the most is realizing that the man I love allowed someone to come between us. He destroyed my trust, and in the process a bit of me. It's like someone jabbed a burning-hot poker into my gut.

This is how I discovered the affair. One Saturday, I was cleaning the house and decided to do the laundry when I saw a bundle of sheets rolled up in the corner of the closet. I have never put our sheets on the closet floor. When I went to grab them, something in my heart told me this was strange. But I stuffed them into the laundry bag all the same and went to the basement. I started putting the clothes into the washer and finally had the guts to take a closer look at the sheets and then I saw the blood. It was menstrual blood, and it wasn't mine. My heart started pounding so hard. I tell you, I thought I'd faint. But somehow my body wouldn't let me. I went upstairs and confronted Ricardo, who denied everything. And that's when the situation really heated up. We were shouting so hard that I lost my voice, and then I just dropped onto the couch and sobbed until my eyes and throat felt like sandpaper. I couldn't eat, sleep, think. I just sat there all afternoon and all evening. And finally, Ricardo came to me, with tears streaming down his cheeks and admitted the affair. And the two of us cried together.

What I did was this: start living as though I was alone. In fact, why do you think I travel so often to New York, my friends? It's not that I don't love Ricardo anymore, it's just that once you've been that hurt ... Do I trust him? I can't answer that. I only know that if the man with whom you've shared the purest moments of your life can slip past the borders of his marriage vows with relative ease, then you've got to start reconsidering your perspective on the marriage. I guess what I decided is this: that the spiritual is more important than the physical. And for me to put such value on our physical intimacy, while he did not, meant that either I should live without him, or change my mentality. And that's how I decided to cope. From that day on my art became more important to me. My art has saved me.

I don't tell anyone today, because it's hard for me to share, but once I dated a man who told me that he had been seeing my best friend on the side. At first I couldn't believe what he was saying, because I trusted him completely. I kept thinking he must be talking about someone else. And then when I finally realized that he was breaking up with me, I went limp. It hurt so bad that for a while I couldn't trust any of my girlfriends. Somehow, knowing that he had been making love to my friend while he was my boyfriend, too, thinking about the rawness of sex and the intimate things that are said between lovers, made me want to throw up. For months, every time I went to the gym to work out, I couldn't stand to see all of us women changing in the locker room. Just the suggestion of nudity got my imagination going full speed. I kept picturing the two of them wrapped around each other. Can it be that we women have become less compassionate toward one another, especially since we have gained more personal freedom? Eventually I accepted the truth. I learned that just because I had loved this guy, it didn't mean he had to love me back.

*Sonia* ⟶ I suppose we all have experienced similar situations. Something I'm not so proud of is one particularly bizarre romance. It began with my first university job here. I was running in circles of extreme wealth and power. I was just out of school, but there I was mixing with the crème de la crème of New York. I had lots of dates. Nothing too serious at first, until I met a financier named Charles. Oh, yes, this guy was a real smooth talker, and he knew how to choose his victims. I was an innocent. I mean, I never had experienced deceit and cruelty, never, until I met this man. But I did sense something subterranean about him, all the same. It's just that if you haven't seen a certain quality before, how can you recognize what it is. After a few years we were an item. I think I was attracted to him physically more than anything else. And he loved to dance. I was drawn to him, I suppose, because we were so opposite. He was brash, a confident, can-do sort of guy, and I was shy. But little by little he started showing more and more of his colors. And, *dejenme decirles*, they were scary. By then I was so deeply involved with him I didn't know how to extricate myself. So I started acting around him. It was a way of protecting myself. I needed time to figure out how I was going to get out of the relationship.

He was the most manipulative and controlling human being I have ever known, constantly coming on to other women. In fact, one night I had invited him to a party and in front of me he picked up one of my guests and left with her. I was almost shaking, I was so humiliated and startled. What a disgusting human being, no? And what about her? She was a guest in my house; I had extended my hospitality to her but it didn't make a bit of difference. She looked at me and laughed when I asked her, myself, to please not go with him. That's the truth.

I didn't see Charles for maybe two or three years after that. I dated other men, but something about him, I will never understand, was still under my skin. And then one night he came to my apartment and pleaded with me to see him, almost knocking down the door, and my landlady had to come and see what was going on. Anyway, I give it one last try.

That night I went with him to his apartment and in the morning, at around seven-thirty, his bell started ringing. It rang nonstop, and I kept egging him on to answer the door, fully aware of what was behind this. It was another woman—apparently he had been seeing someone regularly and she knew he was with me. I felt as though I were in some kind of horror film. Do you know, she stood there and rang the bell for an hour and a half. Then there was complete silence. I looked at Charles's face and he was smiling. At himself and at me, as though I should feel flattered. And then the ringing started again, except this time it was the phone. One call, two, three calls and it continued. Pathetic. I ran out of the apartment that morning as if for my life. And that was the end of my flirtation with dashing, sophisticated creeps. I never felt anything for that man again. And I truly felt sorry for her. Thankfully, I was very young and learned my lesson early on. I guess we don't see other women when we are passionately involved with men. Could that be it? I don't have the answers, except to say we are capable of truly hurting one another, unwittingly and, sometimes, intentionally. Until we are capable of recognizing this not-so-pleasant truth, we can never be strong and mutually supportive.

*Isabela* — I think it is up to us women to be strong and wise, to keep a relationship or a marriage from collapse. That is, if there is any love at all left. I have thought a great deal about this. It seems to me that if a woman really loves her husband and he's having an affair, she can turn the situation around if she keeps her wits about her. Someday, Claire, you may remember these words. I'm not saying it's easy, and believe me, I know a lot of anguish is involved, but think of the alternatives.

I will tell you a story. I had a friend, Cecilia, who had five children, a husband whom she loved, and a lifestyle she had worked hard to create for herself. She had an antique shop that specialized in old clothes, beautiful turn-of-the-century dresses, flapper dresses, items from the thirties, forties, and fifties. The shop was a charming white clapboard cottage on a lake near my godparents' home. Her husband was the mayor of the town. I wouldn't say they were rich, but they were certainly comfortable. The kids were adorable. They were very close. In fact, she and her husband prided themselves on their family life. James was out in the yard every night playing with those kids, baseball, usually. And they had parties all the time for the neighborhood children.

Not far from their house lived a young couple with two kids of their own. The wife, Meredith, was looking for a job as a secretary, and because her two girls were good friends of Cecilia's children, Cecilia offered to see what she could do for Meredith. She talked to James about her and he thought there might be an opening in City Hall. In time, Meredith had a good-paying position in James's office. Several months later, I saw less and less of Cecilia and I saw less of James. Until one day, I was shopping in the supermarket and I ran into her at the checkout counter. She couldn't have looked worse, just terrible. Drawn, thin, white. She was fighting back the tears when she greeted me, and I grabbed her by the arm. She motioned me to wait outside. And then she told me she had discovered that Meredith and James were having an affair. She was so devastated that she was filing for divorce.

You cannot imagine the damage the relationship had on that family. It was excruciating to watch. All of us, friends and acquaintances, felt like doing something drastic, but what? Here were two families destroyed, all of a sudden. I can tell you, I did not look kindly upon Meredith. She could have used restraint. She could have thought about all the people she would hurt by her behavior. Her children were very small, and Cecilia's were barely in their teens.

James ended up marrying that awful woman, and my friend Cecilia took a small apartment with her children. And the kids immediately started having problems. One became terribly ill with a rare stress-related disease, another one was in trouble with the law, a third disappeared—just up and disappeared without a trace. And then James—and I often wonder if it was because of all the trauma—developed a life-threatening heart condition. Five years later, he passed away.

Now, no woman knows how she will react in similar circumstances. But I just can't help but wonder if the outcome of these people's lives would have been different if somehow Cecilia had been able to rise above her grief and save her marriage.

*Sonia* ⟶ If you were educated to be an open and caring person, then you must prepare yourself for betrayal. This is the issue. Does it make much sense to tell children to live by rules, when life crushes those rules to smithereens? How can anyone take wedding vows seriously today? How do you mend your best friend's heart when she tells you her husband has run off with his secretary? Do men *have* to follow their *pinga?* And women. Do they *have* to do one another in? For once I would love to see this: A wronged woman turning the tables on the other woman. By surprising her— not with rage and hatred, anger and bitterness, or recriminations. But with her intelligence. Showing off her grief, every single weary line of it, up close, pore to pore. Without a single tear.

**Luna and Gabriel, I always thought, had such a good relationship. I never would have guessed their marriage could take such a turn. I know that Isabela would say a failing romance is the fault of two people. But I am not so sure. I mean, Luna did her best to make Gabriel happy, always striving to make sure their home was a sanctuary. She nurtured him. And she's strong and indepen-**

dent, the qualities he found most desirable in the first place. So how can Luna be at fault? Or is it that a woman has to be a goddess, perfect in every way, constantly on top of things, never for an instant allowed to be human, allowed to stumble? Marriage doesn't look too good to me, at least in New York City. Too much competition. Too many women competing with one another. Maybe that's it. Women are secretly competitive when it comes to dating. And then again, not so secret about their goals. I know one thing. If I were an opportunist my boss's marriage would be in trouble. He is constantly hitting on me. Always asking me to go to lunch or have a drink, not even attempting to conceal his overtures. Is his wife to blame for his behavior? Isabela would probably answer yes, that she must be doing something wrong at home, otherwise he wouldn't be straying. But if one takes that position, then it seems to me you're supporting the goddess syndrome. Or what Latinas call *marianismo,* which is that women should be stoic, all-suffering and self-denying, like the Virgin Mary.

That's too much to bear for anyone. Absurd. Having to be all things all the time for someone else. Impossible.

# 5

*On the First Week of the Year*

The first week of the year, just after New Year's celebrations, is unusually quiet. The city is still and skeletal, gray and bleak. After the onslaught of parties and chance encounters with friends I haven't seen in years, there is nothing but a long stream of empty boxes on the calendar in front of me, white as the snow outside or the pallid winter sky. *Gracias a Dios* for Isabela.

The phone rings. I get up from reading something not so terribly good—an article in a supposedly hip downtown arts magazine about an actor of the moment—and hear her on the other end. "We all get blue from time to time," she says sympathetically. "Now get your coat and hat on and come over. Luna, Sonia, and Aroma are here. And we're having lunch. The worst thing you can do is stay alone inside your apartment. Okay?"

91

So, without putting on my makeup, I do as she suggests. It's a short distance from my place on Amsterdam Avenue to Isabela's building, but it seems like miles. Each weary step I take is forced back by the wind. Finally, I reach the front door, where the doorman, Enrique, greets me. The broad smile of this kind old Dominican with green twinkly eyes and his *¡prospero año nuevo, muñeca!* lift my spirits. And in no time at all, I'm standing inside Isabela's apartment, which is humming with the voices of Los Del Río, a musical group she says is really popular on the Island.

I see that a large pitcher of Luna's famous eggnog—guaranteed to make you sing the songs of yesteryear, tell secrets, shake your hips to a Cuban *son*—is in the center of the table.

Now I know that this *tertulia* is going to ooze with secrets, secrets that otherwise would remain safely tucked away inside our hearts for quite some time. Luna, in my opinion, always adds a little too much rum to the nog. It won't be long before our tongues are doing the cha-cha-cha.

*Luna* ⟶ Chicas, this New Year's Eve I did it for the first time—I wore yellow panties—they're supposed to bring good luck. At least that's what the Venezuelans think. A friend of mine from Caracas told me so. Well, it's just wearing yellow that counts, really. But I thought if I wore yellow bikinis, I might get lucky twice: Good luck in bread . . . and my bed. What do you think?

**I do admire Luna for forging ahead, even when her circumstances are less than hopeful. I have to hand it to her, she rarely seems to lose her sense of humor, even when she is faced with tremendous disappointment. She would say, "It's faith, Claire, faith."**

*Isabela* ⟶ I think you have more important things to think about than that wayward husband of yours. Like your catering business, Luna. Build it up! When you have good money, I can guarantee you that your way of thinking is going to change. But as long as we're on the subject of romance, again, let me tell you about one fling I had many years ago. It may be hard for all of you to believe now, but when I was young and looking for a husband, the values of my background had such an influence on my decisions that I actually rejected a man who was— with the perspective of time, I can see—my perfect companion. We met at a school party. It was winter. And a college friend had invited me to a dance at a private club. I arrived, *de punta en blanco.* Wearing a beaded beige gown. Silk, of course. In those days I wore my hair in a chignon. I think I must have looked pretty, because some of the men, I remember, whistled as I walked through the entrance. Anyway, I was sipping some champagne when a nice-looking, refined boy walked up to me and asked me to dance. Andrew had a lock of blond hair that kept falling down his forehead. Sort of shy and awkward. But at the same time, *guapísimo.* Extremely handsome. He asked me to dance the rumba. And I accepted. Do you know, his smile was so relaxed, you could see his back molars. True, true. White, very white teeth. And dimples, so deep, you could stuff them with a raisin. Good looking, I tell you. *Un pollo.* Well, we started to work up a sweat on that dance floor. We must have been dancing three, maybe four hours. Then, toward midnight, Andrew asked me to meet him the following Friday. The start of our courtship. It was a wonderful year. But when spring term ended, he invited me to his home in Chicago to meet his parents and that's when my world fell apart. His father was a plumber. When I found out what his father did, I knew that there could be no future for us. Ridiculous, no? At least, these days, that is how I see it. But then, well, my father simply would not have permitted me to marry a plumber's son. I met Andrew one more time at a friend's house and explained I couldn't date him anymore. Oh, my goodness, I feel as though this were happening yesterday. I still have to fight back the tears. I ache to think I did such a thing to that gentle boy and . . . to myself. And wouldn't you know, he went on to become a highly regarded judge. I often wonder what might have become of my life if I had married him. What I would say to anyone who has fallen in love with someone whose social standing is different from one's own is, *¿Y qué?* Just be true to your heart. But on the other hand, I might have saved myself a lifetime of grief. My best friend did marry the man of her dreams. The man who made her heart beat fast. The one who turned her palms into dough and ears into chili peppers. And what happened? She became pregnant with her first child. Then, he says, "You've lost your looks. *Una desgracia.*" And he never, I mean never, had anything to do with my friend again. He took one lover after another, until she had enough and divorced *ese sinvergüenza*. My only regret is that she didn't believe, before she met him, that her life could be fulfilling without a man. If only someone had told her. Preferably her mother!

*Aroma* ⌒ For me, the beginning of the year is always an opportunity to improve myself. Spending those very last hours of the old year and the first minutes of the new one with my family is what's important. Claire, that's something for you to think about. In fact, I would never consider not going home to be with my sisters and my nieces and nephews. Once, when I was in my twenties, I accepted an invitation to a very elegant New Year's Eve dinner dance in Boston. Have I ever told you? Well, it was in a private home, a mansion, and there was a wonderful orchestra. But I've never been so miserable in *all* my life. I was so lonely for my parents and my sisters that I went to my room early and just cried myself to sleep. But enough of this talk about sadness and failed romance. New Year's means new prescriptions, too. I want to know if any of you, and I certainly hope the answer is yes, ate your green grapes on New Year's Eve? I ate all twelve of my California seedless, and I made sure everybody at my house ate theirs. Tart, juicy, and propitious. A chomp and a wish times twelve. All I ever ask for in the New Year is resolve, resolve to do what I want and what I must. And for me, that means a lot more sex this year. I swear.

I have a secret: I also hung a hummingbird. Hummingbirds bring love and happiness to the woman who puts one in her window. They're stuffed, the poor things, into a cocoon of colored paper. *Pero, esos pajaritos lindos tienen poder.* They definitely do the trick—they lead those machos straight to the honey! Really, it works. I went to a *botánica* and I bought *un colibrí.* Now all I have to do is keep my eyes wide open. I know the man I'm looking for will come. *Pronto, pronto, pronto,* let us hope.

*Isabela* — *Piononos* would help you out a lot more than any old hummingbird. What man is not going to come running when he smells a delicious meal? And if I have to say so myself, I think mine are the best. And before you even ask, I've copied down the recipe for you. But first, let me say this on the subject of marriage: Not a single one of us, no one, gets by in this world without a little help. We must support one another. *¡Claro!* Especially when it comes to getting married. Any woman who wants a husband needs friends who show her off. A woman's friends must celebrate her, sing about her, compliment her, make a fuss about her in front of her beau. A woman has to have the help of her friends. Do not forget this. Because most men, I'm not saying all, but most, do not come to marriage easily. You have to poke them. Remember that: Nudge them along. As for the *piononos*, first, I peel three ripe plantains. Then I cut them lengthwise into four slices and fry them in a little olive oil with a pinch of salt until tender. Each slice should be thoroughly drained on paper. Then I make a circle shape with each and fasten the ends with a toothpick. The meat filling is placed inside each circle. After I dip the ends into beaten egg I fry them in olive oil. The meat filling is relatively easy to do. Take a pound of ground beef and brown, over medium-high heat. Add salt. Cook until done. Remove the ground beef from the pan and drain off excess oil. Mix in one chopped onion, one tomato, two hot chili peppers, and one green pepper with one tablespoon of oil and add to the pan. Sauté until soft, about ten minutes. Then add two pressed garlic cloves along with a tablespoon of oregano, basil, one half cup of tomato paste diluted with red wine, one half cup of olives, one tablespoon of capers, and two tablespoons of seedless raisins. Cook for five minutes. Return the meat to the pan and cook uncovered for twenty minutes on a low flame. The filling can be prepared ahead of time and kept refrigerated until you are ready to use it.

*Luna* ⟶ I guess I can tell all of you what happened to me last week. *Ay*, if it weren't for my eggnog, I probably wouldn't, but what the hell. Did I say that? I'm begging all of you to please stay quiet, don't say a word, until you've heard me finish. And Isabela, that goes for you especially. I may be tipsy now, but I am not a fool, or maybe I am; you decide. Well, I received a call from . . . is she a witch or a bitch . . . that Elizabeth. I'm sorry. Apparently she is pregnant with my husband's baby, my friends. My God, what should I do? "Luna," she said to me, "I love Gabriel, and I'm having his child. And even if he never leaves you, you'll never be able to satisfy him the way I can."

**This revelation comes abruptly, but I guess that is typical of life. This first week of the year, when we are hoping for auspicious clues to our days**

ahead, we face an unpleasant quandary: How to respond to Luna's very real pain. There is complete and total silence among us. All we can do, it seems, is stare. But I am thinking I would love to strangle that odious Elizabeth, for hurting Luna so.

# 6

*On Romance*

$\mathcal{I}$ have never had a romantic boyfriend. Most of my beaus have been nice enough, I guess, if you consider men who talk incessantly about themselves nice. But where is all that magic I've seen in movies, a man whose affection manifests itself in the simplest ways? For instance, when he listens to me speak, not because what I have to say is urgent or informative, like a comment about the stock market, but because he wants to understand the way I think, feel, see the world. This is what I can't seem to find. Or what about a spontaneous spirit. "Let's have a picnic, darling. And to heck with your lunch hour. They won't miss you at work if you're back a little late." I'd even be happy to be served a home-cooked meal by candlelight, with guitar and piano playing softly in the background. Something normal and enjoyable.

Oh, I've dated the strangest men. Just last week, for instance, I accepted a dinner invitation from an optometrist. I thought, Well, a doctor has to be pretty safe company. So imagine my surprise—no horror—when he decided to give me a samurai demonstration during dessert. He jumped up from his seat, pulled an Oriental sword from its scabbard, and proceeded to throw it around like a madman, nearly slicing my hand off in the process. I honestly didn't think I'd make it out of there alive.

Poetry, music, soft lights, sunsets, champagne, companionship. Enjoyment of the mild side of life. This is what I can't find in the city. Maybe I have read too many books and seen too many saccharine movies, as my father used to fear. All I know is that city living does little for chivalry. Money, power, more money and power—the mantra of most of the guys I've dated here. The dance of courtship, it seems, can be nurtured only in a kinder clime.

Then one perfectly peaceful April Sunday, I am delighted by Isabela's friends, who assure me that it does exist, this romance thing. "You just have to know where to look," Aroma confides with a cheeky smile.

*Aroma* ⁓ Claire, *lindita*, first a word or two about romance and age. It does get better as one gets older, even though it might be hard for you to imagine such a thing. But as a woman ages, she learns to accept herself. Romance has to do with feeling at ease in body and soul, so that enjoyment can be embraced. Would you believe that the most wonderful period of my life was when I was in my early forties? True! I just sort of blossomed, like some rare tropical flower that comes to bloom every thirty years or so. And I certainly didn't expect it. I had no idea I would find romance in quite uncomfortable circumstances. Very far from home. In Quito, Ecuador.

I had just turned forty-two and had been living alone for a few too many years. It was time for a little adventure in my life. Everything had become stale and predictable. And heaven knows, men were not breaking down doors to date me in New York. So on the advice of my travel agent, Lola, I decided to take a trip to Ecuador. She told me it was really beautiful, especially the jungle. Wild, unpredictable, sensual. Sounded good to me. So, ladies, off I went. Well, I arrived with a small group of Americans and Brits. The first days were a little bewildering. I had never been to an Andean country before, so it took some getting used to— the food, the air, scents, people's stares. But about the third or fourth day I became friendly with a British guy and we started chumming around. We were supposed to spend the first week in the capital before setting off to the jungle. Our small group was being briefed about the dangers, how we should handle ourselves if certain circumstances arose—bad weather, illness, that kind of thing. I was a little nervous, but I thought this was probably the last time in my life I would be game enough for such an experience.

We took a small plane to a tiny village on the edge of the jungle, and there we met our guide, a short Indian wearing a rough woolen poncho and beige muslin pants. He had the kindest, blackest eyes I have ever seen in my life, and thick dark hair that fell to his shoulders. A bandana of hemp was wound around his forehead. I can't explain how I felt when I saw him. It was like a sensation beyond my body but part of us both, like a cord of light that bound us together. I felt as though we had known each other all of our lives. I took one look at him and I felt the sweat trickling down my cheeks. *What was this?* I kept asking myself. We began our journey into the jungle, and when we were crossing a small stream, I managed, stupidly, to grab a very sharp plant of some sort that sent its thorns deep into my palm. I thought I'd die, the pain was so excruciating. Tino, that was his name, came running over to me with the deepest look of concern. And he took some *aguardiente* and poured it over the cuts. The sting was unimaginable. I just let myself fall into his arms as he pulled the thorns out fast, as if it were the most natural thing in the world to do. Then he took a piece of cloth from his bag and wrapped it around the small wounds. He ordered me to take a big swig of liquor. "Go on, please, it will help. You must." I can still hear him saying this, with such a beautiful smile, and I felt so sad. It was strange. I didn't understand why, but in that moment my pain was his. It was as though I saw in him some long and hard road that he was forced to follow, and my feelings were both ethereal and sexual. His Spanish was very limited. He spoke mainly *Quechua*, or some variety of *Quechua*. I could have let myself fallen madly in love. I guess I was surprised; he was not the type of man I would ordinarily have found attractive. Although we were inseparable for the next week and a half—constantly gazing into each other's eyes—I left it at that. It seemed best to imagine what might have happened. How he might have kissed me, held me in his arms.

*Pearl* Once, Claire, when I was in Puerto Rico with my husband, I felt a little touch of magic, a bit of heaven in a totally unexpected moment, as well. That is the key: surprise. Anyway, we were staying in a fairly nondescript hotel, but it had a bar area that was really enchanting, situated within a garden but attached to the main part of the building. So even if you were sitting inside, you were part of the landscape outside. There were tall trees everywhere, lush, flowering shrubbery that took your breath away, a bit of the rain forest at our fingertips. In fact, it had not stopped raining since we arrived, just my luck. But Ricardo suggested that we go have a late-afternoon drink. We didn't want anything too strong, so we asked the bartender to make up something light and tropical. *Cocos locos.* Delicious! And they were served in coconut halves. The problem was that they were too good. I think the bartender spiked them with a little too much rum that day. But at least we were relaxed, and they seemed to lift our spirits a little in that dreary weather. It's depressing when you're counting on sun, sand, and heat for your only vacation of the year, and you're stuck in some small town in the middle of nowhere. In a chill. But that particular afternoon, as we were finishing our second round of *cocos locos,* the gusts of wind not only slapped around rain sheets, but also brought along a wave of birds, lime green and purple, like clumps of flying bougainvillea over our heads, swirling like silk scarves. I can tell you, it was breathtaking. And so, so moody, like a Chagall mural. Because we began to kiss with bird wings in our hair and then we danced a *cumbia.* We were so relaxed at that hotel, my husband even acted like the romantic he was when I first married him, blessed with a heart that's a jumble of maracas, timbales, and guitar strings. Literally. He did something he hadn't done for a very long time: He serenaded me in the bathroom. True. I was taking my shower the following morning, and there he was with one foot balanced on the tub and strumming his guitar, singing my favorite *boleros.* And aren't I a lucky woman?

*Isabela* ⟶ When I think of romance I think of refinement. The finest day, the finest smile, the finest kiss, elegance at just the right place in the perfect beat of time. A dance floor underneath the stars. Music by Villa Lobos.

*Luna* ⟶ My problem is that I am totally attracted to a man who seems to find new ways to break my heart every month. *Ay,* but I do have weekly romance, oddly enough. Do you know what my crazy husband does each Saturday morning? He makes a picnic breakfast for us. He actually makes my favorite crêpes, scrambled eggs with caviar, toast, and marmalade. Champagne. He packs everything in a picnic basket and places it next to the bed. We eat and read the papers all morning long. I love it.

**I can't believe that Luna can talk so caringly about that two-timing nasty of a husband, Gabriel. This guy is not only chasing another woman, but he has fathered her child, poisoning Luna's life in the process, and here she is talking sugar and spice? Someone had better talk some sense into her.**

*Aroma* ⟶ Claire, *amorcita*, buy yourself a hammock. Yes, *hamacas*! I can think of nothing more romantic than an afternoon swing in a *hamaca* near the ocean. Just the pure joy of noodling in a cradle, the sun above you, the sounds of roaring water and your sweetheart getting in beside you, whispering in your ear. Oh, I've had fun in *hamacas* all over the world, I can assure you of that. Especially in Brazil. Once I found a twenty-foot hammock at a lonely beach cafe in Rio and jumped in, closed my eyes, and the next thing I knew a lovely dark-tanned man had jumped in too and started to sing to me.

*Sonia* ⟶ Did you know, Aroma, that the word *hamaca* is Borinquen? It's an indigenous word from Puerto Rico. Claire, *querida,* quit dating businessmen. They are reliably disappointing. What every woman needs is an artist to reinvent her. A musician or a writer or a painter, a man who sees and feels life around him, and who responds to nuance. These are the men who understand romance. Do you know that I dated a painter once who sent me to the stars every time we got together? It was a passionate affair, oh, *sí, sí, sí, sí, sí.* We'd open up a bottle of champagne and then he'd ask me to take my clothes off, which I loved to do for him, because he'd kiss me all the while, and then he'd have me stand on a large Turkish pillow and say, "*Eres una belleza.* And I am going to paint you." And he did! He'd take out some paints and paint on my stomach and my chest and my ankles, all kinds of things: little dragonflies, stars, wicked sentiments in script. I felt so free and adored. I was putty in his hands.

Then again, my Uncle Pepe was not an artist, and I daresay he must have been the most romantic man to ever walk this earth. And I'll tell you why. Each of his and my aunt's wedding anniversaries was spent on an island. Of course, he had the means to make these incredible excursions possible, but how many wealthy men do for their wives what he did for her? I can tell you: precious few. On the eve of March 21, he'd pull from his pocket an envelope with tickets. He would never consult my aunt, just plan everything himself. They went to some of the most magnificent spots. Tahiti, Capri, Bali, Sardinia, Santorini, Corfu. And if all of this wasn't enough, he'd buy her a new gown to take along. Usually something slinky, in velvet or silk from the finest designers.

But none of you, except for Isabela, has mentioned the elixir! The one and only key to romance. And that, of course, is dance. Any one of you can bring out the romantic in a man if you can get him up and running on that dance floor, I promise you. Whatever it takes, I don't care if you have to go to a *botánica* to get some herbs or love potions or whatever they sell in there to get him in the mood. Even if you have to give him a few stiff drinks to loosen him up, go ahead, do it! Do the tango, *el fandango,* do the rumba, or the mambo or pachanga. All that sweat and heat will lead to . . . *amor,* my friends.

After listening to these very sensual, experienced women tell their stories, I feel prepared enough to make my personal romance come true. Before I knew Isabela and her friends I had, I suppose, a North American understanding of the concept. Which, to my mind at least, is much more restrained. A dinner date, maybe a movie. Jeans and a sweater. Now, if I were to apply what these women have told me, watch out!

First, the clothes. Something slinky, a little tight around the hips, maybe. A pair of pointy high heels, thin straps at the ankle. A come-hither attitude. And then there would have to be, obviously, a night of dinner and dance. Dancing. There has to be dancing. Moving those hips and those shoulders is essential. I still can't do it right, stiff as a board, but I keep on trying every month,

113

with their instructions and demonstrations to help me along. "Loosen up, loose," they shout at me, "loose like custard. Look, like this!" And then they all jump into a conga line. In syncopated step, one elbow out, one knee curled high, stockinged feet on fire, smiles. I think I'm becoming more Caribbean in spirit. I dearly hope so.

# 7

*On May Day*

$\mathcal{W}$hat better way to celebrate the first of May than to buy a boutonniere, or fashion a festoon and make a huge bouquet. On the streets I see sharp-looking men with long-stemmed roses, and sexy girls dressed in pale-toned linen suits who are proudly carrying peach blossoms and bundles of lilacs. There goes a guy with one corsage of three gardenias, and that old women seems to be deciding between the lilies and the tulips. To whom will these signs of love and happiness be given? Lovers, mothers, soulmates, special friends?

It seems like such an old-fashioned thing to do, observe May Day. But, oddly enough, the more time I spend in New York, the more sentimental I become. The brass of international business, the lack of courtesy on the street, the rush and shove of daily life have made me more introspective, more willing to search patiently for the object of perfect harmony, gentleness, and inspiration.

I choose my flowers carefully, after peering though the glass cases at Surroundings, my favorite florist. I touch and admire the stacked rows of orchids, butter, eyelid rose, and sand shades. And I marvel at the sumptuous garlands of fruits and vines hanging over me. How about some irises and a few elegant strands of silver eucalyptus added to vermilion roses? This is what I settle on.

There is one person in New York who definitely has helped me through my hardest moments. A true friend. I look at my beautiful bouquet of reds, just like her hair. And, "Oh, please tie them with blue, navy blue, ribbons." Off I go to Isabela's.

I ring the bell and enter to the strains of *"Cuchiflitos,"* a funny song whose title refers to traditional Puerto Rican outdoor food huts, but whose lyrics are about the variants in Spanish vocabulary among Latinos. It is by the great

**Rafael Hernández. We are in a playful mood today, and conversation dwells on the differences in Latin and Anglo sensibilities.**

*Isabela* ⟶ There's a saying, Claire. *Agua por mayo, pan para todo el año.* (Rain in May, bread every day.) And speaking of water, I brought some holy water back from church today, just for you. Since you've been having so much trouble with that nasty boss of yours at work—all that funny business with his *piropos*, his flirtations—I thought you might try sprinkling a little bit on him when he isn't looking. When he's bending over at a water cooler, just throw a little on his back.

The sermon today at my church was about renewal, hope, and spring. I thought the monsignor spoke very well. He is so handsome. I don't remember celebrating May Day in Puerto Rico when I was young, it's true, but I like the idea of celebrating spring with flowers. Look at these bouquets! Have you ever seen such intricate arrangements? And look what Winifred sent me. Narcissi, camass, and double sweet daffodils. Don't you think it was thoughtful of her to do that all the way from Chile?

*Luna* — Certainly it was, but she should have insisted on a few carnations in that bouquet. I love carnations. Red carnations, in particular.

In our house, when I was a child, we always had *claveles* for their clove perfume. But now every time I order a bouquet from a florist, they can't believe it. Carnaaaaations? they say, as if I'm *una loca*. It's as if they're a weed or worse. One day I called a florist to ask that a bouquet of fifty pink carnations, the Doris, Freda, and Constance varieties, be delivered to a friend of mine for her birthday. And the florist said, "I'm sorry, ma'am, we don't sell carnations in this shop. We would never sell carnations. But you can buy them at the grocer's." His arrogance made me mad. Obviously, he didn't know a thing about them. I doubt if he could tell a Dazzler from a Telstar or William Sim or Joker. Although my favorite is Eva Humphries. They look like communion hosts dipped in claret.

**I watch Luna carefully today, wondering how things are going between her and Gabriel. She has been nervously twisting a gold cross chain around her neck all afternoon. I know she went to mass before she came to the *tertulia;* that refer-**

ence about communion and carnations is so typical of her. Luna is a mystery. While I don't really relate to how she thinks, all that religious stuff, I do find her fascinating. Her Catholic faith is so strong, it seems that nothing will defeat her.

I think she is the first person I have ever known who seems so delicate on the surface, yet so steely inside. That has got to throw people off balance. Not just me.

*Sonia* ⌐ I agree with Luna. I like carnations, too, the miniatures especially. White miniatures in thick bunches, to be exact. They symbolize pure and ardent love, you know. Or pinks. The petals are so silky. And the fragrance, unexpectedly lovely for such a common blossom. I think of García Lorca's poetry when I smell carnations. Botticelli's "Spring." Gypsies in Spain selling their bouquets in restaurants and cafes. I think of Cervantes, and Rafael Alberti. *Los hermanos Machado.* Such exceptional poets. *Boleros. Tangos.* Carlos Gardel. Archangels in dark Cuzco paintings. *Sangría,* Valencia, and Las Fallas. *La Pascua.* Good luck. Even bullfights, or church processions and honeymoons. Vacations in San Miguel de Allende. It seems to me that the word carnation comes from the Latin "*carnis,*" which means *flesh.* Like *carne.* What I remember from my reading is that carnations were brought to Spain via North Africa by traders during the reign of Augustus Caesar. The Spaniards always did like pungent, spicy-scented greenery, and the carnation fit the bill perfectly. Doctors used it originally in their medications. And there is a legend that says the carnation was born of Mary's tears, as she stood before Christ on the cross. You know, the pink carnation was always associated with maternal love.

**Listening to Sonia and Luna talk about their passion for carnations reminds me, once again, of how differently we think, although I wouldn't admit to Luna that I feel the same way about carnations as the florist she derided. I would never send a bouquet of carnations to a friend for her birthday. They don't seem special enough. The florist is right, why order them from a flower shop when you can buy them at the grocery store? And yet, as Sonia reminds us, the carnation is probably one of the most favored flowers in**

**Latin culture. Spanish poetry sings its praises repeatedly.**

*Sonia* ⟶ I think of Carlos Pellicer, just about my favorite poet, when I think of carnations. He embodied the spirit of Mexico, no doubt about it. I met him in the early seventies, before he died, because of a strange coincidence at a hotel where I was staying during a literature conference. I remember the restaurant had stopped serving breakfast, and it was far too early for lunch. So I went to the bar, where I knew I could get a good, strong cup of coffee and a roll before heading out to the museums. A small man, smelling of too much cologne, sat down on a stool next to me, and he tried to start a conversation. I moved away, but then he started joking with the bartender about his hundreds of girlfriends and the latest boxing match he'd been to see. Finally, he asked me if I was "*argentina*" and when I didn't answer, he said, "*Eres muy bonita.*" I knew he wouldn't go away, so I told him I was a professor of literature. I thought maybe that would bore him. But he persisted. Finally, I chatted a bit about Mexico City. I mentioned that I loved the work of Carlos Pellicer. "I can introduce you," he offered with a wink. I guess I was skeptical, because he didn't seem the type. But he swore that he was a friend and the bartender nodded to confirm. "So," he continued, "when would you like to meet him? I can drive you to his house this afternoon." Things just seemed to happen like that in Mexico. I have to admit I was nervous, but to meet Pellicer! Of course, I said yes.

That afternoon, Casanova came to the hotel and off we went in his battered Dodge. The car was so rusted, I could see the highway through the floorboard. It took about an hour before we pulled up in front of a low-lying, large rambling house, two sweaty, dust-covered, disheveled figures about to meet the great Pellicer. The house was shaded by some banana palms. I remember the clouds that day were like thin ribbons of tin against blue. Dramatic, almost shocking, the sky seemed. Well, Carlos came to the door himself, and I was thrilled. His cook had even prepared lunch for us: enchiladas with chicken, walnuts, and cream, a thick corn soup with wild mushrooms, and platters of avocado and lemons and fried *nopales*. We ate, the three of us, as though we hadn't eaten for weeks, then we went out back to his patio—which was covered with bright yellow- and white-vined carnations, like a wedding arbor. It was such a beautiful spot, and he had cages of doves. We talked about literature and poetry all afternoon and late into the night. And he recited one poem after another for me.

All the women, even Isabela, are sighing as if in ecstasy. What better aphrodisiac than poetry, they say.

I find myself nodding in agreement and also remembering the first time I went to a fancy Latin American dinner party in New York at which some uniquely lyrical entertainment was provided.

There were eight guests, and I was the only North American. After cocktails, a maid, dressed in starched white apron and black uniform, called us to dinner. When she rang a diminutive golden bell our host, an Argentine industrialist, led us into an ornate dining room filled with old silver relics and ancient Peruvian feather tapestries. The first course, a salad of endive and walnuts with vinaigrette, was served ceremoniously. An hour later an enormous tray of filet mignon followed. Between courses, our host stood up and without further ado began to recite "Martín Fierro," a celebrated Argentine epic. If I concentrate, I can still see him standing straight as a soldier, clearing his throat, and booming out the first stanza. Our host recited the entire work, to my surprise and amused delight. I had to bite my tongue to keep from giggling out loud because he was so earnest in his delivery. But judging from the expressions on the other guests' faces, this was a perfectly ordinary thing to do.

*Aroma* ⟶ I had a beau in my thirties who would always bring me flowers, every time he invited me out. And each time, I remember, he gave me a different bouquet— sometimes a basket of lilacs and camellias and occasionally a wrist corsage. But my favorite was a pale orchid, the petals as delicate as my best French hosiery, jutting from a small black gourd. It was delightful, this Brazilian creation. I remember him, above all other men I dated, as the most tender, the most sensitive. Ladies, don't you agree that a man who brings flowers to his sweetheart has style?

They do agree. And then they launch into a discussion about American men and Latin men.

Hands down, they prefer the latter. American men, they complain, are solely interested in watching television and reading the paper. They lack gallantry. And they're cold. And, rarely, do they bring home flowers to their wives and lovers. They aren't romantic like Latinos. Few of them can move well, let alone dance. They are awkward "boys" who prefer to get down to business, in other words, sex, right away without the preliminary steps of seduction.

All of my dear friends, with the exception of Aroma, reserve their strongest criticism on the etiquette of romance for American women in that category. North American women are far too aggressive, they conclude. Provocative in terribly direct ways. Blunt. They decide that Latinas are more knowledgeable, subtle, in the art of love.

I certainly think that, on the average, Latinas express their sensuality more discreetly than North American women. Is it the way they move, or the way they keep their ardor behind the mysterious mask of their face in public?

I remember watching a three-way flirtation

going on between two acquaintances of mine, one of them a Cuban-American and the other a Midwestern American of Danish stock, and the object of their mutual affection, a wiry American musician. We were in Central Park, having a pic-nic, on a Sunday afternoon. My Midwestern friend was earnestly talking to the guitarist she found so attractive. Everything about her personality was so clearly written on her face. An open face.

But my other friend seemed to hold herself back in an enticing pose. A lot was going on between her and the musician as they spoke, but it wasn't so defined and explicit. Her body seemed like liquid sculpture, constantly curling and uncurling on the grass.

*Sonia* ⟶ Most of the *gringas* I have met in New York are so obvious. And many of them have foul mouths; they can't stop describing their sex lives. Just yesterday I was sitting in a restaurant and a group of them were carrying on and on about the intimate details of their lovemaking, laughing and shouting. What terribly bad taste.

Perhaps, but at least those *gringas* felt free to verbalize their feelings about sex, I say to myself. Without shame. And that, I think, is positive and healthy.

*Isabela* ⟶ Now, Claire my dear, you are quite different from the Anglo women I have known through the years. You certainly dress with more elegance than most. At least you wear skirts and dresses to work, although, for my taste, you dress a little too drably—all that black and gray. Why, you look as though you're dressed for a funeral half of the time. I think young pretty girls should wear color—reds and pinks and royal blues. Especially in spring. And do you ever wear makeup, my dear? You could liven up your features with a nice bright lipstick.

The fact is that I do wear makeup, but a more understated variety than Isabela would use. And I know she thinks I dress far too simply; I rarely wear a hat, something that disturbs her sense of proper form.

Proper form. Propriety. To my way of thinking, Isabela assigns too much importance to these notions. I'd just love to see her kick her shoes off, let her hair fall any which way, and walk barefoot in her house. I tell her the beginning of May seems like a good time to set yourself free.

# 8

*On Mother's Day*

$\mathscr{I}$ see her running in her purposeful way, her left hand clutching a no-nonsense brown leather bag and her right-ringed hand holding a huge bouquet of red carnations. "I'm sorry I'm late, but I've told you to call me before you come over, haven't I? How long have you waited, not long, I hope. Longer than ten minutes?" I answer no, and then I take the flowers while Isabela fishes through her bag. There must be a set of tools, a set of silverware, and her jewelry box in there, I hear so much clanging and rubbing of metal. Finally, she finds it. We take the elevator up to her apartment and as she opens the door and runs ahead, she calls out, "Would you mind making the green salad? I'm not good at that." I hold my tongue. I want to tell her that I'd better make the whole lunch, at the rate she's going. But I don't. "Sure." And then I ask, "How are we going to get the paella ready in so little time? Did you buy the lobster, clams, and oysters, the *chorizo*—the piquant variety—the *pimienta,* the chicken broth? I hope you bought the chicken broth." Not an answer to be heard.

By now she's in the closet, looking for a crystal vase. I look out the large picture window at the garden of magnolias below—a rippling of watermelon pink—and I think about my mother in a far corner of the state. It's Mother's Day and I miss her terribly, her sparkling eyes, the way she calls me honey and her laugh, like getty-up, getty-up. My childhood comes back to me in vivid sounds and shades while I chop the romaine, endive, and cilantro. This is the day of best love, love you always, everything begins with you, Mother.

*Pearl* ⸺ I was pregnant with my first child when I was living and working in Bolivia. I wanted so badly to have a rosy baby that I observed an old custom that seems silly to a lot of my American friends. To us, of course, it is perfectly normal and reliable. I tacked to my walls all the pictures of precious babies I could find. If you focus on beautiful children, yours will be beautiful, too. I stared at each one and wished for my baby to be perfect. And, well, of course he was. But I guess what excited me most about motherhood was seeing how my baby could erase all the ugliness of the world with just a smile. I never would have known how simple it was to focus on goodness if it hadn't been for my Ramoncito. And I guess being a mother enabled me to grow beyond mere hopes of being the best person I could be. It allowed me to attain an understanding of my moral self that I never would have thought possible.

Now, I know that I am capable of doing and being in the most powerful ways. Motherhood has allowed me to dance the *milonga* like nobody's business, *te digo*. But being a mother is terrifying, too. When my Ramoncito was really small I kept watching him grow physically, month by month, with awe, really, but I kept wondering how he was growing spiritually. I kept trying to visualize the pictures he was seeing in his head. How he was piecing together all the horror and the magic of the world. I can tell you honestly that I prayed a lot. I prayed that God, the *Virgen María*, fasten him with love to every goodness on this earth. I wanted him to be strong so that he could always do right, no matter what trouble came his way.

*Aroma* ⟶ Look, the fundamental principle in raising children has to do with giving and listening. Two simple prescriptions for mothers: First, place your babies at the center of your life. They are your jewels. And second, you must listen carefully to what your children have to tell you. And to you, Pearl, and any other woman who has sons, my advice is please, please, please raise them with the same standards as you raise your daughters. Don't make them think that they were born to be served. I see so many women pamper their sons, running to the kitchen to make them breakfast, lunch, and dinner. And they treat their daughters totally the opposite. Why is it that so many women expect their teenage daughters to cook, clean, and look after themselves, but not their sons? They would be doing wonders if they prepared their boys to be as considerate and nurturing as they encouraged their girls to be.

**Aroma, Aroma. What a smart woman. If she and the others knew about all the horrid men I've dated, they would be so angry at me for putting up**

with them, and at their mothers for raising them the way they did. How many men have asked me to cook them a "perfect, delicious meal, right now," at midnight, after a movie, I can't even begin to count. I have seen too many variations on the theme of crassness. My last boyfriend's idea of celebrating my birthday was taking me to a business party hosted by a client.

But no man comes close to being as pathetic as a trader I dated a few times. I should have been tipped off by his very first comment to me: "Hi, babe." We had known each other for all of five seconds, having exchanged glances at an art show opening. When he asked if I'd like a drink and I said yes, he pointed with his index finger at a bar on the other side of the room and said, "You can get one there."

The inevitable call came the following week to invite me to a dinner hosted by his so-called best friend. I asked if I should take flowers. His response? "Let's not get hasty. Why not see if the food is any good first." Then he laughed. Later that night he asked me up to his duplex, "to catch the view." And stupidly I went. On his bureau were black lacy panties and a bottle of perfume. Actually, the room reeked of it. And when I went to use his bathroom, I found someone's diaphragm, just sitting out there, waiting to be used. I kept wondering: Is there an end in sight?

*Isabela* ⁓ What is motherhood but the most precious way to try to heal the world? Some of us do not have children, but we can love the babies of our friends. And we can honor the concept of giving birth, even if we've never experienced it ourselves. All of us give birth in our own ways, *¡verdad!* We create ideas. We bring joy and support to our loved ones. We write music and literature, create clubs and organizations, and we organize activities that inspire and motivate. Motherhood is a flowering of tenderness and strength. Of course, God did not give me the privilege of having children. But I've watched a lot of people raise them. And it seems to me that what children need more than anything is unconditional love with a solid family life and discipline. I don't think youngsters should have unlimited freedom. Parents just have to define limits of behavior and teach their sons and daughters that work is the path to self-fulfillment. Parents who give their children material goods in abundance, without teaching those children the value of working for them, do not prepare their kids adequately for the future. Time and time again, I've seen it. I think where folks go wrong is equating love with material comfort. Children need development, not fancy bikes and expensive trips and all that nonsense. And nowadays too many mothers and fathers think money, money, money when they raise their kids. Look, instead of sending their children away to expensive prep schools and camps that take them away from nurturing, why not show them that they matter *in* the family? I honestly think that where most couples err as parents is in their vision of childrearing. Look, this is a full-time job for at least one parent. I don't care if you hire the best nanny in the world, it simply doesn't take the place of Mother's or Father's undivided attention, at least for the first five years. Children need to feel secure, at the heart of a home.

*Luna* ⟶ I guess for me, Mother's Day makes me think about a woman's beauty. Specifically, my mother's lovely hair. In fact, I can remember everything about it, all the styles she ever wore, its scent of violets, even the barrettes or bands she put into her curls. I remember one New Year's Eve as though it were yesterday, because I loved the way my mother looked that night. Her hair was up—which was rare—and she had stuck an antique rhinestone pin in the crown to fasten it tight.

And lest we forget, please remember La Virgen de Guadalupe today by buying a pink, rose-scented candle. Even though I am not Mexican, I do consider her Our Blessed Mother, too. She does look down upon us. I am certain that she helps us more than we can ever know.

**I think something else is on everybody's mind, though. None of us dares mention it, although I suspect that Isabela would just love to relate some advice. I noticed a huge stack of books about marital relationships on her couch. That's the way she speaks her mind when she knows treading carefully around her friends is required. The matter of Elizabeth's impending delivery. What a mess. I feel sick for Luna. How can she accept the fact that Gabriel has fathered this child . . . and still wish to be married to him? I cannot fathom it. But I guess I shouldn't pry.**

Today I'm also thinking a lot about my own amazing mother. Ever since I was a child, I have known she was a precious human being. She seemed like a fairy-tale princess with her calm, quiet voice and graceful movements. My friends could see this, too. They were forever asking if they could come to my house after school. She was so pretty, and my little friends liked to stare at her as much as I. Beyond all that, we saw that she was loving. A generous human being. She never failed to greet us with giggles and hugs, which made us feel good. And there was always some homemade pastry on the kitchen table—lemon pound cake or brownies or sugar cookies and cold milk.

And I also thank my lucky stars for all the women sitting around me. It is a great comfort to Mother knowing that they have been like aunts to me, each one of them. They have provided me with a circle of support and care that would be the envy of many young women. I truly feel blessed.

,

# 9

*On the Sad Occasion
of an Illness*

$\mathcal{I}$ have just come from visiting my good friend Nina, who is in the hospital, fighting a particularly virulent form of bone cancer. She's the only friend my age with whom I share my most private thoughts. We live in the same apartment building and we've gone through the small-town-girl-in-the-large-city journey together. On this cool and rainy Sunday afternoon I bring her flowers and some freshly squeezed fruit juices from a health food store, apple, carrot, and orange, as suggested by Aroma. But I don't feel well myself. My allergies are acting up. The week ahead holds no great promise as I think about meetings and my routine schedule, and then I feel even more miserable. I walk alone with images of Nina's face, her thinness and pain. I say a prayer. "God, allow her some rest, some comfort. Provide her with your strength. Please heal her."

I must admit that while I do believe that the Almighty is listening, there is a bit of doubt within me. It's hard to think positively when there are so few signs of Nina's recovery. I can't stand to see her suffer. No matter how much morphine or Demerol is administered, she still cries out in pain.

So many relatives and friends in recent years have been afflicted with cancer. I often find myself looking at someone who is vibrant and healthy today and wondering if some new health problem is waiting to erupt.

All I know is that I need to talk in order to rid myself of lingering antiseptic scents, pristine cleanliness that speaks of distance rather than human warmth, alarming bells, and orders barked from overworked nurses doing what's expected of them, nothing more. In fact, when I start to analyze the hospital personnel I met while visiting Nina, I realize that it's just a job for them. They come, they go. They get paid, go home, and try to forget . . . for their own health and sanity. And I understand that. I feel so discouraged.

When I finally reach Isabela's door, I'm in tears. No, it's worse than that. I've cried so hard, my throat is raw and I can barely breathe for all the pollen in the air. Isabela is far less emotional than I am. To lend perspective on the matter, she tends to take the conversation from an immediate, soft spot to somewhere far off in the distance.

*Isabela* ⌒ Nothing can uproot the personality of a loved one like a serious illness. But I'm afraid, Claire, it's a part of life. Several of my best friends have had cancer, too. I'm certainly no biochemist, but I can't help but think that a lot of this misery comes from stress and an unsettled life. It seems that I know so many women who've gotten sick after a major upset or a huge letdown or a disastrous romance combined with some really serious financial trouble, some kind of disappointment that seeped into their hearts and made them vulnerable. Remember this, my friends: A woman has to listen to her body, come to recognize the emotions and thoughts that make her healthy or, *al contrario*, throw her off balance, and then do everything she can to protect herself. And not just from illness, but also from doctors, who can make matters worse instead of better. And buy books! As many as you can afford—on prescription drugs and their side effects, on alternative medicine, on disease, on the latest treatments available.

*Sonia* ⟿ Neither one of you is alone. I have two friends who are waging all-out war with cancer, with such grace and dignity. It has brought out the strength in them, and an instinctual struggle to survive. But to be a witness to someone's suffering? *Te digo con toda sinceridad,* Claire, I don't know what to do, either. I can't find the appropriate words or gestures to convey how I feel, not even in poetry or great works of literature. I end up feeling totally useless. And then I experience extraordinary anger. I want to run away and forget. But when I'm about to abandon these two dear friends—for fear of being hopeless—I remember something that a colleague, a philosopher, said once to me: "Food, flowers, holding hands. These are real gifts for the grieving."

*Pearl* ⟶ In my youth, Claire, it's no secret that women were more apt to listen to what a doctor had to say, usually a male doctor, without questioning him, then follow his instructions to the letter—even if, in her heart, she knew that he didn't appreciate a thing she had to tell him. I've had so many encounters with doctors who would roll their eyes if I asked for a particular treatment I might have read about or just laugh, truly, in my face when I told them what I thought was wrong with me. That's right. Well, those days are over; I've learned to be a juror in matters of my health. If my doctor doesn't respect my views, I get up from my chair and leave. *Se acabó.* No doctor is going to intimidate me. That's right. Life is too precious to be fretting and scared silly in some dark and unfriendly, sterile office with a *macho* physician who couldn't care less about my feelings.

During one illness, and I know that Isabela remembers this well, I kept a diary outlining my symptoms. And when I decided to go to the doctor for treatment he ignored what I had to tell him. He did a multitude of blood tests. Fine. But then when I tried to work with him, he shut me up. Mind you, I had done a lot of reading about my condition and I had some definite ideas about medical therapy. I thought I was rather well informed.

But he got so mad that he saluted—he actually got to his feet, did an officer kind of thing with his hand—and showed me to the door. When I got outside, I burst into tears. I could hardly walk home. I was so miserable that I almost decided not to seek treatment at all. That is how strongly his attitude affected me. Quite deplorable. And then, thank God, a friend of mine referred me to an acupuncturist. That woman, a lovely doctor from Korea, changed my life. I remember her office was so clean, the walls luminous. Milky, with a sheen that lit the air. I entered feeling defeated, but she put these very small, fine hands on my wrists as though she were praying and then she listened to me. She was so soothing. I relaxed, and I really started feeling better that very afternoon. I guess it might sound strange, but it's true. Knowing that she cared about my thoughts, not just wanted to give me a drug and send me out the door, changed absolutely everything for me.

*Aroma* ⟿ Please don't count me among those doctors who run a factory kind of office. Some of us, perhaps most of us, really do care. One of the reasons I wanted to become a gynecologist is that I believed I could help women heal in ways that most of my own doctors scoffed at when I was young. Pie in the sky, feminist fluff, they used to call it.

I met a young Costa Rican artist when I was in college who told me a story that convinced me that healing is more a matter of metaphysics than pure science. Apparently she had been working to complete an enormous number of artworks for an exhibition. Staying up all night, not eating well, sleeping just two or three hours. Well, her show was a success, but the day after the opening she told me she lay in bed in near paralysis. When she tried to get up, the room began to spin. She had absolutely no energy. She stayed in bed for a few days, only getting up to drink some water. Finally, she was able to move around, but she realized that she couldn't talk. The months of tension, of grueling work, had knocked her out.

She sensed that what she needed was a mammoth source of energy, a current to ignite her well-being. And so, a few days later, she took a bus to a fishing village on the coast. There she took a room at a quiet inn. She walked the paths along the sea, inhaling the pine and salt air, which she loved. She spent hours gazing out to the horizon, played in the sand, gathered shells and twigs, and let herself become a part of it all. "The aquamarine around me," she said, "was an antidote to my collapse. I concentrated on the color, then I visualized the sky and sea within me, cleansing my body, washing out my exhaustion, like a gigantic stain."

At the end of a few weeks, she could speak. This made entire sense to me. And since then, anytime I've had a patient who believed she needed more than my prescriptions, I've told her this story. And I've encouraged her to go on nature trips, to help along the healing process.

*Pearl* ⟶ Most of my doctors are women. It's not that I think they are necessarily better physicians, but they tend to be better healers. They say, "I know what you're talking about" or "Yes, I felt that way when I was pregnant." We speak the same language. No need for some mysterious translation in the office. It feels easier, better, somehow. And the nurses, the staff, in the offices of my women doctors seem different, too. The curtains in the dressing room—cheery flower prints! One doctor even hums songs while she takes my blood pressure. Soft, fluty chants about faith and hope and the power of the Divine to heal. In a *reggae* beat. *Ay, sí.* She moves on tiptoe, nearly gliding. The first time I met her I thought she was an angel. She made me feel so calm, I actually *enjoyed* being there. It made me feel whole and safe. No stuffy, scary seriousness or a sense of doom. Would you believe, her waiting room holds a museum-quality display of international dolls?

*Luna* ⟶ I will never forget a remedy of an old *curandera*, a healer, I met when I traveled to New Mexico, after I found out about Gabriel and Elizabeth. I didn't mention this trip to you before; it was a sacred act for me. Anyway this *curandera* was like a little sapling, thin but strong looking, with the greenest of eyes. She was sent to me by the hotel concierge. Not only did I lose the rhythm of my life, but I lost all of my confidence too when Gabriel told me about his affair. I felt quite worthless, if you have to know the truth. Nothing made sense to me anymore. But all of you know that I am trying to cope as much as I can. Well, I found this lovely old adobe-style inn just outside of Taos and decided to try to be as open as I could to everything, especially the energy of the landscape, the mountains, the people. I wanted to try to heal and refocus. One night I was eating dinner alone when the concierge stopped at my table and said he had a small surprise for me. He must have seen that I was in pretty bad shape.

That night, at about eight-thirty, the *curandera* came to my room. At first, it seemed she was a spirit, a vaporous being, light and radiating light. But she smelled of the earth, dry and sweet, like roasted corn, and kept whispering, "*tranquilo, tranquilo.*" Then she walked around the room and set up all kinds of candles, white candles, and as she lit each one she murmured words I found unintelligible. Sighs, she almost sung. She asked me to sit down and then she disappeared into my bathroom.

I heard the water running. Ten minutes passed, I'd say, and then she stood in the doorway, beckoning me to come to her. She placed her hands upon my shoulders and then she walked past me while saying, "Please, please take a bath." And then she left. Well, all of this was so unusual but at the same time immensely comforting. I walked into the bathroom and there, too, were many lit white candles. Next to the tub she'd left a muslin robe, hinting of lavender, with a scribbled note to put it on after my bath or "*baño.*" As soon as I got into the water, I felt as if I were unfolding, like a long bolt of silk. I think it was the openness, cleanliness, and quiet that had already started to lull me. But the water itself was therapeutic. It smelled delicious. Now, whenever I feel depressed, I draw a bath similar to the one that night. Sage and rosemary, wedges of lemons and limes, marigolds and peppers, all floating on the surface, like a springtime broth. I went to see the *curandera* in her home a few days afterwards and she taught me some medicinal recipes that I still use, too. She mainly worked with herbs from the country-side and the mountains, and those she found along small streams. *Oshá, yerbabuena, romerillo, berro,* many kinds of wild flowers and tomatoes, *piñón, orégano, nogal, nopal, mostaza, maíz, cilantro, chili,* and *uña de gato.* Old herbal medicines. She mentioned that their origins were North African. And because of Moorish rule in Iberia, they were handed down through the years to Latin America. Probably the best advice she gave me was to take *uña de gato,* cat's claw in English. Now I buy it in powder form at the health food shops. She knew all kinds of applications for the flower and the leaves. "*Corazón,*" Ana-Belén said, "it's good for everything."

*Aroma* ⌒ I tell all of my patients to eat lots of water-cress. It's good for healthy kidneys. A purifier. I think it's good for the entire system. And oshá, from the parsley family, is a divine medicinal herb, with the power to heal and protect. It is truly the forgotten equivalent of any modern-day supplement like echinacea, good for almost everything. All of you should put oshá leaves in your broths and sauces. If ever any one of you feels anemic: make a tea from its leaves. It's really good for sore or irritated throats. I'll give you some next week, Claire.

**Isabela has a few special recipes of her own, some might call them nostrums, for colds and flus; a bit unorthodox, you might say. And she loves to remind me that there are just as many excellent therapies from Puerto Rican country doctors for my allergy affliction as there are expensive pills made by pharmaceutical companies.**

*Isabela* — Claire, my dear, you could get rid of all sniffles and coughs if you'd only follow my advice. A trip to Puerto Rico is in order. Once there, you must find a particular hummingbird: the Puerto Rican emerald. Quietly, very quietly, on tiptoe, follow the emerald back to its nest. Although it's not a nice thing to do, you must grab the nest, which is made of cobwebs, and take it home. Then, very carefully, burn it until you have a small ash pile. Mix the ashes with boiling water, as if it were a tea. Sip slowly.

The matter of good health is an issue that we talk about quite frequently. But for the *tertulia,* it could be very easy to forget about eating nutritious foods, getting exercise, resting the mind, in this megacity—the heart of the universe—because the reality of the street, the glitziness, the grandeur, the sparkling imagery of expensive shops and high-powered festivities, seem constantly to say that everything is just fine. The New York scene can fool women my age into thinking about the surface only. Nina's illness puts an end to that for me. But how to live? What example do I follow? Probably, Isabela's admonition—"Claire, keep your feet on the ground," coupled with enthusiasm for simple living—is a fairly good way to stay healthy.

# 10

~

*On Travels Far
and Wide*

*E*ver since I was a little girl I dreamed of traveling to faraway places, to lands of snow-capped mountains and liquid skies, to picturesque European villages and mystical sites in Asia and the Far East. I floated to those places in my reading chair, and I think my father worried greatly about the power of my fantasies overshadowing the grit and struggle of life. He would shake his head and lament, "She lives too much inside her head." My mother used to tell him not to fret so much because she intuited that I was meant to travel. She knew this when she held me in her arms the very first time in the hospital, just after I was born. For lack of a better way of interpreting this understanding to my father, she likened her knowledge to an energy she felt in me, the energy of imagination.

And she was right, but my father had a good point, too. I have had some close calls on my journeys, probably because my head was in the clouds. But what they don't know is that I've traveled to the farthest places in my heart and soul. It's not just the wandering that takes us to the outer reaches of our world. In fact, I think the most beautiful place I've ever been was in a dream once. And I can remember approaching a window in a sacred place, something like a church, but not quite, and the window was divided into many, many smaller windows, triangular in shape. The room was white, except for just a few tall candles here and there, and as I approached that window, my eyes grew wider and my heart grew fuller at the sight beyond. There were thousands of lights like small stars, hanging on trees, navy, green, purple, and aquamarine. Curtsying trees. And the lights kept multiplying on the side of this great mountain. It was a land more breathtaking than any I have seen. I felt billowy and free, just like a kite, moving through celestial spheres.

**At this particular *tertulia*, we are thinking about summer vacation, and exotic travel is on everybody's mind.**

*Aroma* ⌒ Ladies, if it weren't for travel, I don't know how I'd get by in New York. The pressure of this city, I admit, is just too much to bear without some breaks. And I do recommend getting away every five months or so to all of my patients. Travel promotes good health. So a favorite prescription of mine for any patient is: Travel three times a year. My all-time favorite trip was the excursion to Antarctica I took last year. Do you know, I haven't enjoyed a trip more. A cruise that took us through the milkiest of water and ice floats under a blazing sun. Everything was pearly and aglow, like being in a fairy tale. A steward on the ship was busy cutting ice chunks off glaciers that we passed. He carved the ice with a pocket knife into small goblets with long ice stems. Honest, they looked like Waterford crystal. Each passenger received one for sipping champagne.

*Sonia* ⌒ I had the most traumatic experience of my life on a trip. I suppose I should have known it was coming, because somewhere in the deepest level of my consciousness, I knew my companion was a horror. There are no words to describe the meanness, I mean pure baseness of this guy. And what on earth was I doing with him in the first place? *Chicas* . . . he was sexy! But I learned a lesson . . . never to forget. You have to take your time getting to know a man before you become intimate. Otherwise, your heart will be served as brochette.

We went to the Dominican Republic for Easter one year. Both of us needed a vacation, after a grueling winter of exceptionally hard work. So we were looking forward to this little excursion. When we got to the airport, we decided to rent a car. We wanted to see a little of the countryside. So off we sped into an apricot afternoon, deep within incredibly lush vegetation, smoky and mysterious, scented with goat barbecue and corn. I started to unwind.

The next day, after we had spent the night in a lovely hacienda-style hotel surrounded by flowering trees, we decided to take a look at some remote sites. I was in charge of the navigation. Omar did the driving.

After traveling maybe six or seven hours we reached a fork in the road, and I was confused. The road was badly marked and I couldn't find it on the map. In fact, all maps there were terrible. Anyway, Omar asked, "Well, Sonia, which way?" And he was so nasty, so imperious and demanding, that against my better judgment, I just chose blindly, without knowing. So I said, "Go left." And we did, and we got farther and farther away from where we wanted to go, until we reached another town. And when we came into the little plaza—I remember there was a lovely blue and white church on one side and a small restaurant on the opposite side of the square—his face turned maybe five shades of eggplant. And he lit into me until I was trembling. And he didn't stop. He yelled at me to get out of the car and he actually sped away, with me standing on the curb . . . shaking. And I realized that at least I had my bag with me, with my credit cards, and I planned to run to the restaurant and call for help, so I could get on a plane that afternoon and go home to New York. And so I ran to the little place and as I was talking to the operator, in marched Omar and he continued to yell at me. By then I was so unraveled I thought of escaping, so I went into the bathroom. And, my God, a flood, an inundation came welling up inside of me until the flood became a rush of water from eyes, my nose, my mouth. I had never cried like that in all my life. Never, I promise you. And when I had somewhat regained my composure I went back out and tried to eat. He was the closest thing I've encountered to *el diablo*. And he just sat there and stared at me with the coldest eyes. Of course, I couldn't eat. And I would say that within fifteen minutes of that moment, I came down with a flu, a fever, I don't know what it was, but I was so sick, I thought I'd die.

The rest of the trip was pretty awful. But that moment was seared into my memory forever. And to this very day I think of that horrible man. Vile. And I can tell you this: I will never again travel with a man until he proves himself in a hundred ways to be kind and gentle. In other words, I will never travel with a man again, until I marry.

*Aroma* —— Sonia, that's ridiculous! The best way to get to know your beau is on a trip. How else would you find out what he's always hiding from you? *Mira*, on a controlled date, such as dinner and a movie, you never get to see personality traits and habits that could absolutely drive you crazy in a relationship. *Sabes* . . . his habits in the bathroom and in the bedroom. In fact, I make it a point to travel with my lovers right from the start. That's how I was able to prevent a disaster from happening with an Uruguayan architect

I was crazy about. *No quiero ser grosera, pero* . . . do you know what this elegant, well-dressed and -spoken man did in our bedroom on our first night in the hotel? He sat on the bed, took off his socks, threw them in the air, and proceeded to pick his toes, one by one, while he watched the news.

*Pearl* Now, I am remembering an interesting trip I took in college. I took a semester off and traveled throughout Latin America. At that time, in the seventies, there was so much political unrest. People were frightened and nervous. Students were marching everywhere to protest one outrage or another. But it was just at that time that I had one of my rarest encounters with art. Great art. Because I had been involved with international student affairs at college. I had met a lot of influential, wealthy alumni who lived abroad. And one guy, a Venezuelan statesman, invited me to spend some time in Caracas. He thought I would enjoy learning a little about his culture.

When I arrived at the airport, I was surprised to see him and his wife. I hadn't let him know which flight I would be on, only that I would be arriving on such and such a date. But, you see, he was extremely civil, very well mannered. And his wife! She was as gracious and as beautiful as the Duquesa de Alba. Truly! There they were, dressed immaculately in navy and pearl white, the two of them waving at me as I came through the doorway. They grabbed my bags and led me to their chauffeured car and away we went through a maze of highways. Finally, after what seemed an interminable journey through dark streets and alleys, we arrived at a small hotel. Very pretty. With etched-glass windows giving views onto a park. Once my host and hostess saw that I had been given a comfortable room—actually, it was a suite with a cream and beige sitting room and a pale blue bedroom—they said that they would be by the next morning to take me to "the club." I'll tell you about the club another time. Anyway, that first night I slept as though I hadn't slept in a week. In the morning, when I went down to the small dining room, I was impressed by the beautiful paintings on the walls. Magnificent reproductions of Van Gogh, Monet, Matisse. Actually, I was mesmerized, because the artworks seemed so authentic. When I went to pay the bill, a distinguished man with beautiful wavy silver hair walked in and greeted me. "Miss Pearl," he said, as I was about to leave. I turned abruptly, thinking that I must have known him, but a good long stare proved not.

"Yes," I said, quite unsure of myself, "have we met, I'm afraid . . . forgive me for asking. But, I'm sorry . . ." "No, absolutely, not. We have not!" he boomed in a jocular manner. And then he went on to say that my politician friend had told him all about me. Well, we fell into conversation. And I learned that he was the owner of this hotel.

We talked for maybe fifteen, twenty minutes, when I realized it was time to get going. My hosts would be arriving at any time. But before I left, I asked him about the reproductions. I wanted to know who had done them so expertly. "But, my dear," he replied, "they are not reproductions. I'm afraid they are the real thing." "But, these are Van Gogh, Matisse!" "Yes, quite. This little restaurant is the safest place I can think of in this menacing city of ours. No one, no one would ever imagine that they are authentic. And that, simply, is how I prevent their theft. Clever, don't you think?"

*Luna* ⌒ For me, travel is a rare form of prayer, a way to find the divine in this world. And now with my troubles with Gabriel, I really wish I could get away more often. Routine so clouds the extraordinary qualities of our friendships, our work, and our homes. I can't help thinking that, *ay*, if Gabriel and I had taken more trips together, none of what has happened would have occurred. Maybe we would have appreciated each other more. I only know that traveling has a way of making us more aware. And that is the beginning of prayer.

**I can't stop cringing when I hear Luna speak such nonsense about her marriage. It seems to me that she keeps blaming herself for what has happened. When will she realize it wasn't her fault that Gabriel cheated on her?**

*Pearl* —◦ What I like most about traveling is the colors I learn to see that I never knew existed. Traveling is essential for my art. I, especially, love being on a boat or near the ocean. That's right. Water is the greatest life force. Striations of heaven. I swear, I could live on a houseboat for the rest of my life. Just watching water. Just painting the secrets of water.

**Pearl is passionate. And when she talks about primal forces, she is truly captivating. She has a gift for examining, absorbing, and comprehending**

the world around her, an ability of all true painters. When Pearl describes water I see a special place—Mosquito Bay in Vieques Island, off the coast of Puerto Rico. Whether you describe its poetry or its bare physical properties, it seems to embody otherworldly qualities. In scientific terms, the bay's enchantment would be attributed to dinoflagellates, a kind of phosphorescent plankton, also known as pyrodiniums. A lyrical description, I suppose, would be to say that the universe had brushed against the water in an act of love, producing liquid starlets for our enjoyment. The simple truth is that on a moonless night, a swim among the "whirling fire" waves inside the bay could be the most spellbinding experience of your life.

I walk out of Isabela's apartment convinced that if I took a short vacation in the next month or so I could thrive in myriad ways.

# 11

*On a Christening*

Elizabeth's baby, a boy, was born on a late August day of insufferable heat. She named him Edward, according to some avid gossipers who know Isabela. Whoever would have thought that the birth of a gurgling infant could be the cause of so much despair and pain in one woman's life. Apparently the child is being christened as we speak, this September Sunday.

None of us at the *tertulia* can figure Luna out, none of us, that is, except independent, mysterious Pearl. She hasn't said too much about Luna's decision to stay with Gabriel. But I have a hunch she approves. Meanwhile the rest of us are pulling out our hair. Could she possibly think he loves her still? After all that has happened? I, for one, can't believe it. And what about Elizabeth? Surely, Luna hasn't heard the last of her. In fact, it seems to me that she will always be a part of Luna's marriage. Why has Luna consented to the intertwining of their destinies?

We have come to Isabela's table ready for this brewing debate, to try to understand what Luna's thoughts are on the issue and persuade her to do the right thing. If she asks for my advice, I'll tell her to take the next plane out of New York. I think she should make a clean start, for God's sake, somewhere else. Washington, D.C. might be just the place. So many swanky embassies, and many more diplomats with sophisticated palates who continuously host dinners parties and black-tie affairs. Luna's catering business would really take off there.

*Luna* — I'd like to say grace today if Isabela doesn't mind. I'd like to air some thoughts. So, dear God, before we eat this meal that Isabela has prepared for us, I ask that each of us walk carefully around each other, talk carefully with each other and listen. Allow each one of us the sensitivity to accept what is. Open our hearts. Amen.

Now, I know that all of you are looking at me with

round sorrowful eyes, as though I've lost my mind. But I want you to know that I haven't. And I will explain, I will, I promise.

*Sonia*

> *Ye happy shades, whose deeds renown'd*
> *Have freed you from encumbering clay;*
> *From this low scene where woes abound,*
> *Ascending to eternal day.*

From *Don Quixote*, in case you didn't know. Who better than Cervantes to catch the shadows of our sorrow. I read Cervantes every day. *Quixote* is my bible.

*Aroma* — *Por Dios*, Luna, think this over. Think of your mental health, my dear. Any self-respecting woman would have left Gabriel months ago. You deserve a better man. A man who knows how to love, really love you, cherish you. *Mujer*, a prescription for your mind. Let go of that piece of *chabacano*.

*Pearl* — Well, let me say that I am certainly glad I flew in yesterday. Otherwise I'd have missed this lunch. *¡Que div-*

*ina comida!* Now, it might surprise you all that I am totally in favor of Luna's decision to stay with Gabriel. I am. I think that Luna finally figured out what strength is all about. It's not necessarily acting the way that makes sense to millions because they've bought into conventional wisdom. Should we agree with pop psychologists? Self-appointed gurus on marriage and relationships? I should hope not. In fact, I find it alarming how easily so many women allow themselves to be, how do you say, bamboozled, by some authority who is making a fortune on her opinions and spreading them around as if she were the end-all and be-all of appropriate behavior. Many of us are nothing, nothing but little girls acting as women. Going to this expert or that expert to find out how we should behave when we have problems. Too many women have abdicated their creativity of thought and mostly out of laziness. That is why so many of us fall when hard winds blow. We haven't built our own foundations. Foundations, I might add, that are as different for each one of us as the color of our lipsticks. I think, *con toda sinceridad,* that Luna is brave and incredibly strong. And smarter than the rest of you. And if I were to paint a portrait of her at this very instant, it would be in yellow, gold, and bronze hues. In honor of her enlightenment.

*Isabela* ⟿ Well, *vieja,* I disagree with your painting of things. Not that I don't think Luna is brave or strong. That's not the point. What is important is that she is going to have to live with the fact that the man she calls her husband has fathered a child with another woman. What does that make Luna to that child? An aunt, a stepmother, a second mother, a foster mother, a second-hand mother? And there is another matter to consider. Her catering business. All along, I've said that this is what Luna should be focusing on: making a success of her talents as a cook. How can she focus on such a priority if in the back of her mind she's thinking about Gabriel, Edward, Elizabeth. Now is the time to put herself first. She has to if she wants to succeed. *¡Pues, claro!*

*Luna* ⟿ So, here is where I stand. First, while all of you know me, you do not know the me that is the me-with-Gabriel. It's a mistake for any of us to assume we know each other that well. Of course, I've cried, laughed, talked, and even worked with you, but there is a part of myself that I reserve for me alone. A person whom none of you knows. Now, when Gabriel first told me about Elizabeth, I felt a horrifying betrayal. Such pain that, I had no other recourse, but to leave him. Remember we talked last December about it. I could hardly make it through the days I felt so torn, depressed. And then, of course, worse news: hearing from Elizabeth she was having Gabriel's baby. I have to admit, that although I am a religious woman, I felt such hatred toward that human being that I was scared for my soul. *Ay,* it's true. There is more. About a week after Elizabeth called to give me "her news," I found a letter she had written to Gabriel. He had left it on his desk, right there, out in the open. I couldn't help but notice that letter. Pink stationery and perfumed. I started reading. And I kept on reading. And I felt as though there was a fire in my stomach, I was so humiliated. I don't know what things Gabriel had told Elizabeth about me, but my God, that woman knew no shame. Truly, knew no shame. She was trying to persuade Gabriel to leave me. And she kept on telling him he should not feel guilty. Guilty over what, she wrote. I tell you, I had never in my life felt such anger.

This was the turning point for me. Feeling such searing hatred. Oddly enough, I didn't feel that way about Gabriel. That is when I truly knew I still loved my husband. His behavior had done nothing to diminish my love, which I know might be hard for all of you to accept. But I did feel confused. I simply couldn't understand how the man I loved and trusted could hurt me so deeply. It was impossible for me to comprehend. But getting back to the issue of hatred. What nausea. What ugliness I felt and saw around me. I started crying one day and I couldn't stop because I finally learned what my limitations as a woman were. And then came knowledge. Real knowledge about me. And then came the desire to be better than I was. And I knew I simply had to forgive. Forgive Gabriel, forgive Elizabeth. How did I forgive them? It came simply. And strangely. While I was making an almond cake. It was as uneventful as that. Without the slightest hint of what was to come, I just felt peace. Real peace, when I suddenly accepted what was: that for whatever reason, a reason that I would never understand, Gabriel chose to sleep with this woman and there was nothing to be done about it. But that was their story. Not mine, not Gabriel's and mine. But theirs.

Now, the baby. When I knew that Elizabeth would have this child, I sat down with Gabriel one evening and asked him how he felt about it. I was surprised and startled. *Ay, sí.* Because he reacted in a way I simply wouldn't have predicted. He told me that while he wasn't happy about her decision, he also wasn't unhappy about it.

What, truly, concerned him was how I felt. He couldn't bear to hurt me anymore. He wanted to know if I could forgive him for what had happened. He still wanted to live with me. And he offered more. The truth. He told me, I imagine, what he thought I could bear to hear. And he also promised that whatever issues would arise in the future, because of Edward, he would keep, truly separate from us. In other words, *desde este momento en adelante*, from this very moment, there will be a kind of measured honesty between Gabriel and me. I can live with that. You might not, but I can. Of course, all of this works on the condition that he keep his promise. That whatever future entanglements he has with Elizabeth, they be solely regarding Edward, and whatever financial responsibility he bears for him. Their affair is over. But Gabriel's and my life has changed forever. On reflection, maybe not for the worse. Who knows what the future holds for us.

I have thought a lot about little Edward. And his mother. Instead of defeating me, her behavior has had just the opposite effect. Now I want to be a better woman, a stronger woman, a more successful woman. And I have surprised myself. I am joyous for the first time in a long time. I am finally feeling relief. I wish Elizabeth and her baby nothing but health and contentment. And so, a toast. To the happiness of a newborn, to his tenderness, to his future. . . . And, Isabela, I *choose to* make a success of my business. Don't you worry.

Luna may be able to forgive and forget. But I don't think I could. Everytime I think of that afternoon when I saw Elizabeth and Gabriel, walking arm in arm, I feel sick to my stomach. That image stays with me. Maybe not having actually seen them together has, in some ways, protected Luna. Everybody else though seems to support Luna's decision, however reluctantly. I just hope I never have to socialize with Gabriel in the future. I don't think I could fake that everything is cool. What does make me happy, though, is seeing Luna so determined to make good on her catering business. I think she now has the unwavering strength and self-confidence to make a success of it.

# 12

*On Beauty*
*and Conquest*

When I hear that Winifred is arriving from Chile to spend a few weeks in New York, I rush around the antique shops downtown, trying to locate a little something special for her. She is an inspiration. An opera singer and a landscape architect, and successful in both careers. Remarkable for the way she interprets the world around her, as though reality were nothing but unfolding wonder. In her presence, the day becomes a celebration of sound and light.

It's late in the afternoon when I invite her to my apartment. "What do you think I should do with these tall ming trees?" I ask. "And what about the ferns and the mock orange in that corner?" She stands erect in her beautiful wool suit, her silhouette illuminated by the blood-pink light falling on the Hudson. She is an elegant diva onstage who takes a few steps back until her gaze takes in the living room, every wall and niche. At first I hear a melodious trill, the register changing in a flash, and suddenly her lovely humming rises to a punctuated high, "*Sí, sí!* Of course!" Gliding down the steps into the sunken living room, she takes the smaller pots of green and places them together. Then she takes one palm and puts it in the opposite corner on a table, by itself. "Now, the eye will fly from this point to the other, creating a line that both connects and separates the area, making it larger and intimate at once." Why did I not see that, I think, as I listen with the transfixed gaze of a child hearing her mother read a favorite bedtime story.

The next day is Sunday. Winifred is holding court at Isabela's. And we are listening to a story, a story about love, loss, power, and adventure. The kind of tale that North Americans just don't often hear. One that is also culturally ambiguous. It involves a woman who, at best, was extraordinarily brave, as brave as any man, and at worst, as violent as any warrior. It is a tale that holds the keys to so many mysteries about the continent of South America, the clash between civilizations, the isolation caused by inhospitable terrain and extraordinary natural barriers like the Andes range, the melding of indigenous and European sensibilities, the struggle for power among few, the great division between rich and poor, the contradictions of class. And the tenuous station of women, their seductive power over men and their subservience to them.

*Winifred* ⟶ I suppose the most interesting landscape I have designed is a national park in the mountains, just outside Santiago. I never thought I'd learn so much about my country and Pedro de Valdivia, Chile's founder, while envisioning the garden. But an even bigger surprise was my discovery of Inés de Suarez, his lover. I might have heard of her, but she didn't take hold of my imagination until I started my historical research and came upon a description of her in a rare book. Then I went to the library and took out every volume I could find about Valdivia and Inés. And it didn't take long to learn that in no uncertain terms, Inés was co-conqueror of Chile. You simply can't imagine how heroic this woman was. Her life seems like fiction.

It all began in Peru, in 1539. Inés, by all accounts, was a gorgeous creature with guts. She had just made the torturous journey from Spain via Venezuela in order to find her husband, a soldier who had traveled to the New World in search of fortune. But there, Inés was told that he had died before ever reaching shore. Rather than return to a lonely existence in Spain as a widow, she was determined to continue on alone. When she finally arrived in Cuzco, the government officials took pity on her. They gave Inés a house, some servants, and a little property.

One night Valdivia was gambling in a tavern when he spied a woman in a long black lace mantilla walking by. Fate struck with the pitch of lute and psaltery. Captivated by the flame-haired beauty, Valdivia approached her gallantly.

*Isabela* Has anything changed? *Pues*, what man doesn't like a good-looking woman, or maybe I should say sexy-looking woman? Even my Argentine butcher, Luis, stares at every pretty girl who walks into the Colorado Market. It's embarrassing, I tell you. Embarrassing.

Although I think the notion of sexy-looking is complicated. *La dicha de la fea la bonita la desea.* (An ugly girl's charm is a pretty girl's desire.) At least from what I've observed of the women coming and going at 14K, next door, I'm sure that what appeals to this skinny professor neighbor of mine is probably my cousin Esteban's idea of a very plain girl. He likes women who are buxom, blonde, and big-boned.

*Sonia* — Can it be that a woman is as beautiful as her imagination? If she's smart enough, she can make herself into a star just by dreaming loveliness. What's inside can and often does come to the surface.

*Winifred* — *Preciosas*, may I finish my story? *Pues*, Inés de Suarez was a sensual woman whose mission in life was to suffer and struggle. Her beauty seems to have been of very little use to her, really. I would like to think that somehow, through the spirit world, she called me to remember her.

I think it could also be said that she was a seer. Inés possessed an extraordinary connection to natural forces, not just intuition, but something more, *un no sé qué*. And she was a source of endless giving, whether it was in the way of material goods or her passion or her loyalty. Valdivia could not have vanquished the Indians, nor could he have launched his campaign through the Andes, without her.

She began her partnership with Valdivia by selling all her jewels so he could buy his ammunition and supplies, red wine and grain.

*Sonia* A perilous mistake already. Selling her jewels. She should have kept them for her own time of need. Women simply can't afford to part with pearls and amethysts. For one thing, there is nothing like a string of pearls to bring poetry to a lover's lips, and if a woman is blessed with a long, slender neck, believe me, those lustrous pearls will inflame his intentions. Speaking of pearls, did you know that in ancient times they were swallowed just like vitamins, in order to promote long life? It's true. Especially in Japan.

But getting back to the subject of beauty. I don't think it has to do with, *digamos*, a straight nose or full lips. No, no. It's the energy of a woman that enhances her physical characteristics. What makes a straight nose crinkle or lips smile is the way a woman's intelligence acts upon the world. Oh, when I was in my late teens, just starting to date, there was the most beautiful woman in our town. *Guapísima*. In the classic sense of the word—the planes of her face, and the space between her features, were, well, so judicial. And it wasn't that her eyes, nose, and mouth together made for a stunning picture; each feature was refined. Especially her hair—a kind of auburn, a color you just don't often see. Men used to stop and stare. Even more astonishing is that she was as gentle as she was lovely. Anyway, she was married to a nice-looking guy. Pleasant face. I don't remember what he did. Eventually, the word was out that her husband had left her for another woman. A woman who in fact was not the least bit pretty or, for that matter, personable. To be honest with you, she was the kind of woman most of us dislike. You know that old Andalusian belief in the *mirada fuerte*—that ferocious stare that men make when they see a woman who turns them on? *Pues*, she did that to the husbands of her friends, without the slightest trace of shame. So, you see, this issue of beauty that we focus on doesn't mean much in the way of contentment. I've always thought that intellectual curiosity gives a woman allure. Beauty and age go hand in hand. We grow beautiful in equal measure to becoming wise. Really, the hard part about birthdays is not aging, but losing our courage. When that happens we fade away. Which reminds me of these Nahuatl lines:

> *Sólo con nuestras flores*
> *nos alegramos.*
> *Sólo con nuestros cantos*
> *perece nuestra tristeza.*

> *Only with our flowers*
> *do we make merry.*
> *Only with our songs*
> *does sadness disappear.*

*Winifred* ⟶ *Oye*, Sonia, thank you, dear, for your insight and your recitation, but, please, may I continue? Well, just imagine Inés in her gear and her wardrobe, a mix of Old World and New World—Extramaduran velvet, the finest in Spain, and the thickest Peruvian llama wool. Her hair dripping with sweat and sand, sometimes snow and ice.

The journey was arduous and wretched, alternating

with the scorching heat of desert and the boot-breaking ice of the Andes, mile upon mile.

The men, overcome with thirst and hunger, and delirious, were falling to their deaths. Inés singlehandedly saved them. She had noticed a horse going wild near a cactus. And gathering her strength, she approached to see that he was feeding on a kind of bulbous growth. It was the prickly pear. She pulled off fruit after fruit, lacerating her hands, and immediately distributed the small, hard pears among the men.

Would it surprise any of you to know that again she would reveal her divining skills? One day, as if obeying the agonizing cries of the soldiers, she stopped and squinted at the white sky above her. They were in the desert and the heat was stifling, and there was no hope of water anywhere. Wiping the sweat from her face and neck with the tattered hem of her skirt, she forged ahead and grabbed an Indian servant while pointing to a spot in the earth. As she dropped to the ground, she ordered him to dig. The others surely thought her mad. As the sun reached its zenith, the men were writhing in excruciating pain. A strange darkness soon surfaced around the servant's ankles and began to flow like mercury. Inés lay her face upon the scorching sand and cried. What had she discovered? An underground well. *Y, oye*, this oasis still exists today, you should know. It retains the name it was given at that moment, Jagüey.

Her gift to perceive not only objects and the wonders of nature, but also the character and the bent of Valdivia's men, was not to be outshone by a gargantuan physical strength. She was a crazed warrior in the face of her love for Valdivia, not only saving his life but saving the lives of them all. Her single most astounding act would confound and confuse even Valdivia's most beloved soldiers.

During a particularly fierce and bloody battle, it seemed as though the Araucanian would bring the Spaniards to their knees and obliterate Santiago, their small village. Valdivia was with a small group of men far from the settlement, hoping to cut off any reserves the Indians might manage to provide their warriors. It fell upon Inés to strategize and form a battle plan. Realizing the enemy was getting bolder in proportion to the battle cries of their seven chiefs, whom Valdivia had managed beforehand to capture and imprison, she sought to quiet the fount of their inspiration once and for all. What did she do? This vixen first chose the best coat of mail she could find. With a force that caused her knuckles to pop, she fastened the metal sheath tight to her bosom and ran to the Indian chiefs' holding cell. There she demanded that the guard do his duty, but he only stared blankly. Not having time for his fussy bewilderment, she grabbed his sword and, racing forward, swung the solid silver blade over her head, and with all the force her weight could bear, she thrust downward, killing one chief, then another and another. When the last *cacique's* head rolled in the sanguine pool around her, Inés de Suarez strode off in triumph in command of all Valdivia's troops. The settlement was saved.

I feel nauseous. Honestly, I can't believe what I'm hearing. Could any woman really do this? Have the power, let alone the inclination, to whack off seven heads? Centuries later, this story seems confusing, at least from my perspective. Certainly, the prowess of Inés as warrior is extraordinary. But it also appalls me. I want to believe that women are more inclined to seek peace than satisfy a lust for blood. I can understand that she, by necessity, had to think of self-protection, but I guess I'd like to rewrite history here. I would prefer to think of women as negotiators.

*Winifred* ⟶ And after all she endured, my friends, Inés would not be permitted to remain with her beloved Valdivia. For you see, back in Spain in a whitewashed house, alone and lonely, was Valdivia's long-suffering and abandoned wife. Upon the ceremonious decree of the Spanish king, Inés was ordered to marry Valdivia's best friend, a man for whom she had little affection, if she wished to remain in the New World.

*Isabela* ⟶ Here we have a case, a perfectly awful case, of a woman who could have achieved a happy life for herself, Claire, but who chose instead to follow a man. And where did it get her? She had intelligence, ambition, an adventurous spirit, and beauty. And she ended with nothing. Not even love. And I daresay that it was her beauty that brought upon her terrible woes in the first place. *Ay, bendito.* When will women learn?

*Luna* ⟶ Beauty plays games with women. It makes a fool of us, if we aren't very careful. And not a few of us are its slaves. We pluck eyebrows, lift weights, peel off skin with creams and gadgets and nonsense made from God knows what. And beauty can come between friendships in the strangest way. It causes envy. *Más y más celos.* That's what I believe. No matter what we might think about makeup and exercise and beautiful clothes, while they might make us feel better from time to time, they don't make a bit of difference in the ways of love. When two people get along, it's not because of what they see, but what they *imagine* they see. And, of course, this is a matter of temperament and energy. We'd be very foolish if we thought otherwise. A painful truth that I have finally embraced.

*Sonia* ⟶ Don't you agree that the best way to think about beauty is to imagine it as separate from us, a gift to others? Nothing more, nothing less. It doesn't assure us a thing. Neither love nor companionship. *Es un regalo.* A gift. If I spot a lovely face on the street, I think: *Now, there is a remarkable design.* But rule number one: The best way to deal with our own physical beauty is to forget about it. You know, I've been thinking a lot about Pablo Picasso lately. Specifically, I've been wondering about the portraits he painted of his lovers. There is an eternal quality to their beauty. There are two I find especially fascinating, though: one of Dora Maar and the other of Marie-Thérèse Walter.

You know he painted them in the same afternoon, apparently in order to compare them, understand how and why these women attracted him. While on one level *me da asco*, this business of his many women, it also makes me wonder about his need to be desirable. Obviously he needed to prove repeatedly that *he* was the beauty. *¡Qué monstruo!* Yes, a monster.

*Isabela* — Well, all I can say is that I pity women who think a face-lift will solve their problems as they grow older. First, because they subject themselves to pain and the knife in order to grasp what's fleeting anyway, some kind of abstract physical ideal. Second, because they fall into the hands of men who have done a very good job of making money out of women's insecurities, insecurities that they have fostered and nurtured. And third because, at least in the cases I know, every time a woman has a face-lift she loses some characteristic that is wholly hers, a kind of grace. *Sí,* a kind of grace. How can I explain? Well, one example is a friend of mine who got rid of her smile lines and the lines between her eyes. Now she looks perpetually startled. It's as though she has never learned one single thing in life. Her face is so tight, it's painful to look at.

I wonder if Isabela is talking about Estrellita, a Brazilian friend of hers. That Estrellita is obsessed, it seems, with her body. I know she is at least seventy years old. I couldn't believe what she did one day when she was visiting the *tertulia*. She grabbed me by the arm, pulled me into the kitchen, and confided in a whisper that when she's on the beach even young men admire her figure. And then, without any warning, she dropped her sundress to the floor and said, *"Niña,* have you ever seen a body like mine? Not bad for an old lady, eh?" I have to admit I was startled by her lack of modesty. She was completely nude, no panties or bra. And she had shaved herself all over, and I mean all over. But, incredible as it may seem, she had no wrinkles, not a one, anywhere on her body.

*Winifred* ⁓ Actually, I've always thought a face is much like a garden. As a garden matures, it unfolds. The foliage may become thicker or thinner, the colors richer or paler, the blooms and shrubbery, which with time alter space, make shadows. Greenery changes in time. But is an old garden less beautiful then a new one? I should think not.

I look around me at these women I love. The conversation returns to Valdivia and Inés. Hands up in the air. In between our chattering and gestures, we are savoring Luna's exquisitely flaky, beef and olive turnovers and her absolutely superb *papas à la huancaina*. She uses little blue potatoes, and her version of the peanut-buttery pepper sauce originating from the town that gives the dish its name is, simply, out of this world. Our meal is complimented by a chilled Rioja.

It seems that each of us relates to different aspects of the tale about Valdivia and Inés's journey. Luna is wondering about the food. What did those poor souls eat? And what kind of wine was served to the soldiers on the trail, a port, or something thinner, tarter? She doesn't mention anything, *ni pi ni pa,* about the love between Inés and Valdivia. And let it be. Aroma is completely fascinated by the menacing features of their path.

The terrain. The desert, snow, and formidable Andes. What kind of landscape greeted the couple when they peered down the Mapocho River valley for the very first time and saw what would be their new home? Her eyes are glowing. Maybe she is thinking about another trip. And Pearl. Well, Pearl has the most vivid imagination of us all. She says she'll paint a portrait of Inés as soon as she gets back to Arizona. It will be a large painting, floor to ceiling. Mainly white. Yes. Many shades of white. Pear and ivory, beige and linen. Sonia wants to know where she can buy some books about Inés. She wants to include her in a course she is teaching. Maybe, she pauses, she should even write a biography of her; there is nearly nothing in the canon regarding Spanish women of the Conquest. And she hastily points out a fact to Aroma: *"Recuerda,* many conquerors came to the New World to find new medicines, not only gold and silver. Imagine that!" Of course, the *tertulia* wouldn't be complete without dear Isabela and her admonitions. I feel a tapping on my shoulder and then I hear the skipping of her voice as she begins, "To Claire, I make an appeal: Please be careful if or when you choose a husband. Be smart. Investigate the man with whom you fall in love. A woman can never, ever, be too careful. *Caras vemos, corazones no sabemos.* (Faces tell one thing, hearts tell another.)"

More than four hundred years have passed since Inés de Suarez proved herself to be a match for adversity. She was an operatic protagonist, maybe not entirely likable or understandable to women of today. But she appears to have done it all. She was wife, adventurer, lover and companion, financier, conqueror, nurse, cook, and spiritual adviser. She might have had children. And still, so few people in Chile or South America, let alone the United States or Europe, know about her strength and courage. She appears in so few history books. Winifred did extensive research before she even came across a brief summary of her life. I'd like to think that in death she turned into a snowbird, beyond the Andes mountains, hovering over the earth in peace.

I leave Isabela's house this balmy afternoon

and think about the goals and passions of my friends. We are looking for success; that's the truth. The kind of accomplishment that makes you feel as though you've taken your life and made the most of it, as though you have striven to complete yourself. I think about my own future. I have a good education and enough ambition. And I found out last week that I was accepted to law school. Working so hard for almost nothing these past five years forced me to confront the truth: the discipline of law challenges me in an exciting way. But I've decided that I don't want to be *just* a lawyer, like the ones for whom I've worked. I want to be better. I am going to study international relations as well as law, so I can fulfill my dream of becoming a diplomat, the dream I had in college. I was visiting a friend in California, just sitting on the beach and watching the ocean, when I realized Pearl is right. Something about the water's calming power helped me to think more clearly about my desires.

I know many educated women with abundant

drive but little opportunity for adventure and the kind of risk that leads to self-fulfillment. A few friends, most of them artists, have to waitress to pay their rent and eat, and they seem particularly worried and frustrated, or confused. Even with a college education and a job, they need to seek their parents' financial help or ask for a loan from their boyfriends. Some can't afford to go to the doctor. One friend survives on hard-boiled eggs. Another hasn't seen a dentist in years. My friends tell me they can't bear to depend on the generosity of others to get by. They feel weak and humiliated. I always try to lift their spirits, though, just the way the women of the *tertulia* have always lifted mine. I tell them not to give up, not to succumb to despair. Even when they think that all is lost, I encourage them to imagine something better in the future. And as far as asking for help, financial help, well, sometimes that takes far more strength than not asking. It is hard to be humbled.

Power, I believe, comes from loving who you are. And this is where I see a lot of hope: Isabela and her friends. Their stories have changed the contours of my life. Their ritual, their Sunday afternoon *tertulia* of telling, of putting their experience into words, has been, in a way, an ongoing chant of protection. These women, from so many different traditions, bound by the same language, bound by ancient Spanish song, have a gift for hospitality that extends beyond the satisfaction of a delicious meal. They have opened doors to truths I hadn't thought about, made me see so many possibilities where I saw obstacles. Their stories have made me think that beauty comes from acceptance of everything, taking in pain as well as pleasure in whatever way you can, allowing yourself room to grow. I will never forget the lessons of transformation they have shared. Isabela's apartment is, and always will be, a holy place for that reason.

I try to reassure Isabela that I won't fall in love with someone who will hurt me, leave, or discourage me. "You just don't know," she keeps repeating as she shakes her perfectly combed head and takes her glasses off to look at me squarely.

Of course Isabela is right; I don't. But I've decided that at least I am prepared for heartache. I know that there will be times when strength will fail me; there are for everyone. But I also know that I will persevere. Should I lose my orientation along the way, I will find my path again. Isn't that where all of us begin? With doubts and questions that force us to discover for ourselves what we are about, what we must do, then keep on struggling, praying, loving, dreaming, and forgiving.